The
INNOCENT'S
Story

The INNOCENT'S Story

Nicky Singer

Holiday House / New York

For Edmund,
fearless companion on the journey,
with my love

© Nicky Singer (2005)
THE INNOCENT'S STORY was first published in 2005
by Oxford University Press in the United Kingdom and
first published in the United States in 2007 by Holiday House, Inc.
All Rights Reserved
Printed in the United States of America
www.holidayhouse.com
First U.S. Edition
1 3 5 7 9 10 8 6 4 2

Library of Congress Cataloging-in-Publication Data
Singer, Nicky, 1956-
The innocent's story / Nicky Singer. — 1st ed.
p. cm.
Summary: Thirteen-year-old Cassina Dixon narrates her existence
after being killed in a terrorist bombing, when, as a "para-spirit,"
she passes through a series of hosts, including the bomber and
the religious zealot who would force him to kill again.
ISBN-13: 978-0-8234-2082-7 (hardcover)
[1. Future life—Fiction. 2. Faith—Fiction. 3. Terrorism—Fiction.
4. Fanaticism—Fiction. 5. Death—Fiction.
6. Supernatural—Fiction.]
I. Title.
PZ7.S61728Inn 2007
[Fic]—dc22
2006030017

1

Okay. This is what I think happened: I got blown up. Boom boom, explosion, Cassina Dixon, aged thirteen, is blasted limb from limb. I'm not trying to be funny about this (a characteristic of my father's) but to try and explain it, if only to myself. You see, I'm not quite the person I was at 5:11 p.m. yesterday afternoon. In fact, I may not be a person at all.

Perhaps it would be helpful to return to some sort of beginning. The pivotal point could have been my mother saying, "Would you mind picking Aelfin up from gym club, Cassina?" Doesn't sound like a death sentence, does it? In fact, as requests go, it has to rate pretty high on the innocuous scale: just walk your sister the ten minutes home from school. No big deal, and not like I hadn't done it before. Besides, Mom had a good excuse: she's a teacher at Aelfin's (yes, I know it's a stupid name, we'll come to that) school and it was parents' evening. It's not wise to cross my mother on the morning of parents' evening, not her best mood day. So I didn't say, "No, I won't pick her up, the little squirt, because I've got better things to do," like homework (yeah, yeah) and a life to live, not to mention some urgent texting, I just said, "Sure, I'll get her."

You should see Aelfin in her gymnastics outfit—well, navy blue Lycra leotard, actually. She's eleven, Aelfin. I have the word *was* trembling on my lips, (incidentally, "lips" is purely metaphorical as I don't have lips anymore)— Aelfin *was* eleven. Who would have thought so much could change in twenty-four hours?

Anyway, Aelfin is (was) blond and willowy and supple and incredibly athletic. She turns somersaults like that's what God put her on Earth to do (not that I believe in God, you understand—we'll come to that later, too). When Aelfin mounts the horse she could be flying. She wins prizes for her antics, so many it's begun to annoy the other mothers. I don't mind about the prizes; she keeps them in a cupboard with the door wedged shut. You actually have to ask to look at them.

"Do you think I could look at your knickknacks, Aelfin?"

She has cups, shields, medals, certificates, and ribbons. She doesn't even smile when you look, just opens the door a crack, gives you a glimpse, and then snaps it all away again. Hardly gloating, so it can't be the prizes that annoy me about my sister. Besides, I was never into gymnastics. I'm too big, too fat, too uncoordinated. And I have pimples. Or used to. That has to be an advantage of my current situation. I no longer have pimples. Hey—let's celebrate.

Mom always said I had a tendency to ramble on, to digress, maunder, expatiate, whatever. She also said, yesterday morning: "Don't stop anywhere on the way home." She said this because I have another tendency—to drift into music stores—and there's an excellent little CD place at the train station halfway between Aelfin's school and home. A CD store just begging you (as you're passing anyway) to drop in and spend a little of that birthday money that's weighing down your pocket. And as my birthday's irritatingly close to Christmas (thinking about it, I'm so glad I got my birthday in before this happened), you don't have long to wait for renewed funds. Anyhow, I picked

Aelfin up as instructed (got there a little early, just in time to see her execute a perfect sky-dive and double twist pirouette, impeccable two-foot landing, and shy, engaging smile), made sure she had all her gear (she can be a little spacey, our Aelfin), and set off for home.

"Just going to pop in here for a sec," I said as we passed the station.

"But Mom said . . ." Aelfin began.

"Yeah, yeah, but who's taking you home today? Me. And I say our route lies via the station."

"But I'm hungry."

"Fine. I'll get you a pastry."

The price you have to pay for a younger sister. We got the pastry first. A cinnamon Danish—her favorite. That was a mistake—not the Danish but the fact that we went to the bakery first. If we'd got the CD first, all this might never have happened. We'd have been in the right place at the right time, instead of the wrong place at the wrong time. So if one's attributing fault (which, of course, I'm not), you could say it was Aelfin's stomach's fault, or my flawed generosity. You could also say it was to do with me disobeying Mom, but I'm not sure even Mom would hold that against me under the circumstances.

Right, so—we got the Danish and adjourned to the CD store. Aelfin munched in her irritating way (how come she can eat so many Danish pastries and still look like a pencil, anyway?) while I checked the latest hot hits. I'd like to say that, at the time of impact, I was clutching to my breast the divine Robbie Williams, but of course I wasn't. I was just replacing some tacky *Hits* album that had fallen off the shelf. In fact, that was my first impression of the explosion: not the noise, not the screaming, but movement. The CDs beginning to rumble and jump. Now, of course, the explosion must have happened first and only then can the CDs have begun to jump. But that's not how I remember it. The CDs were definitely jumping first. And then there was the noise. Noise is a bit of an understatement. There was what they call in the papers a "deafening bang." It's quite a good expression because although the noise was certainly louder than anything I have ever heard, there was also a weird kind of silence as if my ears had been overloaded and decided to cut out. So the noise had the quality of seeming far away and not at all to do with me. So much for the brain in a time of crisis.

The CD in my hands fell, of course, but as an entire rack of CDs was falling on me anyway, that didn't seem to matter too much. Then there was the sound of glass shattering, as if a million windows popped at once. The window of our store had the virtue of being sucked outward, so while we were certainly being hit by all kinds of flying objects, we were not, mercifully, being shredded by glass. Not then anyway. I guess that's when I actually got to look at Aelfin. And you know what? She looked terrified. I actually put my arm around her.

I tried to say, "Let's get out of here" (Smart thinking, eh?), but no words actually came out of my mouth. It was as if all the air had whooshed out of my lungs. Not out of everyone's though. Some people were screaming. Really screaming. Later I thought, maybe these were the ones not really hurt. Anyhow, I pulled Aelfin toward the absent door (read modern sculpture of twisted metal) and out into the concourse. If I'd been thinking, it would have been about the open space and the decreased likelihood of falling debris, but actually, of course, I wasn't thinking; I was just acting instinctively: station—bad; out of station—good. Or, put another way: Let's run, Aelfi!

Only we didn't run; we ambled. I'm not sure whether that was because we were injured, or shocked, or simply waiting for someone to tell us what to do; because there's always someone, isn't there, telling you what to do? "Get behind the cordon, move on, not this way, please, line up, sit down, shut up." Did you see the first images of the Twin Towers falling in New York, when they just replayed the building falling, falling, again and again, rerunning the disbelief? I kept waiting for them to say who was behind the attack, or what it meant, but nobody did because nobody knew. And I realized then that normally everything comes to you packaged, people tell you what to think, frame events for you. Well, here were Aelfin and I and no one was framing the event, it was just happening, exploding around us, and we were walking it as if in a dream.

Anyway, we were out on the concourse, not so very far from the ex-entrance of W. H. Smith's. Then it happened— Aelfin fell. I didn't see her hit by anything, and nor was I hit (not then, anyway) but she just fell, even though I thought I had my arm around her. And then she lay there, on the ground. She was quite still, and her body was arranged beautifully: one arm above her head, the other tucked in behind her waist, her back and legs a graceful curve. Her head was half turned to the concrete, her hair falling lightly across her cheek. She didn't look hurt at all; she might have been a ballerina, playing the part of an exquisite bird resting after a long flight.

Not that I had much time to look, because something did hit me then, whacked me in the back. I can't say, even now, what it was, only that it was hard, angular, swift—and painless. I hope it was like that for Aelfin. I didn't lose consciousness, but my consciousness changed; I felt all parts of my body slow, my mind was quite calm, and I experienced myself as much less involved than only a moment before. It was as if my perception had moved from participant to observer. I didn't feel any regret, or even any surprise, I just felt slightly airy, slightly lifted up.

I'm not sure how long I hung there, in that quivering,

hovering state, probably only a few moments, though it was sufficient time for me to view the whole station panorama. My main thought was that people were rushing too much, that they ought to slow down, there was no need for so much frenzy. But that was mainly the outer ring of people; the inner ring, near where the crater was, was more still. There were people lying there, some quiet, some twitching just a hand or a foot, as if they were cold, or nervous. Which is why the coming of the man was so strange. I should have seen him immediately, because he was standing, and no one else was, not at the edge of the crater anyway. He was covered in dust, perhaps that's why I missed him at first, stripped naked by the blast but so stuck with grime he might have been just another piece of debris. Then he moved, lifted his hands in front of his dirt-brown face and stared at them, as though he couldn't believe his own palms, the existence of his fingers.

After that he lowered his hands very slowly and began to walk, away from the inner ring where the fallen were and toward the outer ring. He didn't look right or left, didn't pause at all, until he came to Aelfin. Then he stopped and stared at the position of her body, at her half-turned face. A terrible shudder seemed to pass through him. It sounded to me, so close above him, like a door banging in the wind, only I think the door was his heart. He flung himself over Aelfin, then. Didn't drop to his knees or touch her lightly, but threw the whole force of his body over hers as though he might be able to protect her, shield her. And she never moved, for she was dead. At least, I think she was dead.

What happened next I didn't see because that's when I began to be taken up. I say "taken up" as though someone was pulling me, but actually it was rather the reverse. It was as though I was being pushed, as though someone had thrown a switch and reversed gravity, and there I was spiraling into space. No, *spiraling*'s the wrong word, it wasn't as fast as that; it was more floating, hazy. I'm pleased to say there still wasn't any pain, although I did experience the cold, the higher we got. *We.* Afterward I thought there should have been a "we," because it wasn't just me knocked about down there, so there should have been plenty of us floating upward, but I think it was only me. Not that I felt alone: being pushed into space was so unlike anything I'd ever experienced before I wasn't about to shout: "Hey— what about the others?" I was just busy with the business of movement, of keeping whatever was left of me together.

Of course it occurred to me that I must be dead, too, but then I didn't feel dead. I still felt pretty much like myself, like Cassina, so I went with the flow, didn't even feel cross or resistant. As I've spent most of my thirteen living years being cross and resistant, I guess this supports the being-dead theory. "No, I won't tidy my room. Why should I? It's my room, isn't it? Yes, sure I'll float up beyond the known universe, why not?"

I'm not sure how many miles, or thousands of miles, high I was when I realized that the floating sensation was probably to do with the fact that I had no body. You'd think you'd notice, having dragged around this large, bulky suit-case all your life, if it parted company from you, wouldn't you? I suppose that supports Mom's view that I always lived "too much in my own brain for my own good." I don't know exactly whose brain she expected me to live in. But here's the question that's bugging me: If Aelfin's body is lying neat and intact on the station concrete—what precisely has happened to mine? Okay, perhaps I shouldn't go to that place; perhaps it's enough to be grateful that I've become this sort of mist. Yes, that's what it most feels like; I'm some sort of shapeless (no change there, then) mist. I belong together but I'm formed of tiny malleable particles.

But I'm running ahead of myself (well, not *running* exactly, due to the absence of legs) because, on the ascent, I thought I was mainly brain, or mind anyway, didn't notice myself as a physical presence at all. It was what happened at the top that changed things. I had a sense of "arriving;" not because the landscape changed much, or St. Peter burst through some pearly gates exclaiming, "Cassina, what took you so long?" but because I began to slow down, like a train does when it approaches a station. I felt it as inevitable that I was going to stop as it had been inevitable that I had been propelled upward. And although, as I've said, I'm not a great one for believing in God, I was expecting a welcoming committee of some sort. Because *someone*, I reckoned, must have wanted me somewhere other than that station concrete, or why all that pulling or pushing? No such thing as a free flight in space, right? Wrong.

I did stop, I remember that; the agreeable feeling of being at rest, of having arrived. But what was my destination? A starless galaxy, high and dark and cold and spacious. Not unpleasant, merely vacant, absent, like a universe that hadn't been born yet. It felt like being inside some cosmic tinderbox that was patiently, oh, so patiently, waiting for a spark to bring it to life. It occurred to me (grandiose, I know) that maybe I was supposed to be that spark, that that was my purpose, what I'd been sent for. You'll see a theme here, my constant expectation that *someone's* in control, in charge, that things have to have meaning and purpose. More than that—that *I* have a purpose, and that, in this case, my purpose was to switch on this new universe much as a celebrity might switch on the Christmas lights on Oxford Street. Well, that's not quite how it turned out.

I'd only had a moment or two to scan my new playground and think my grand thoughts, when I fell.

"Fell" would be a bit of a mild description. I plummeted, I hurtled, I vortexed in a downward direction. Someone (here we go again), *something*, reversed the gravity switch. I whirlwinded about. This is when I realized I must have a physical presence after all because I could feel myself being sundered, driven apart. The little, wettish particles which had followed me on my upward journey like some gloomy cloud were now following me downward, only now they were spinning apart. I was spinning apart—and that was painful. Imagine yourself in the drum of a giant washing machine, only instead of water being wrung out of the holes, it's bits of you. So I had to grab for myself, centripetal myself, call all my little droplets together. It gave a whole new meaning to my father's favorite phrase: "Pull yourself together, Cassina." I pulled and cajoled and begged myself together, and eventually—eventually—the drum stopped turning.

But I didn't; I still felt like I was revolving. But maybe I was evolving: Cassina Dixon, solid thirteen-year-old hominid becomes small, exhausted patch of mist. Mind you, considering what happened next, that was the good news.

2

It took me a little while to work out where I was, never having been in such a room before. But at least I was in a room, which implied "Earth," a comforting beginning even if the room was cold and full of coffins. Well, not full exactly, there were only two coffins, but they were the ones that counted: mine and Aelfin's. Mine was a light, attractive teak and, on the screwed-down lid, a brass plaque announced: Cassina Melrose Dixon. Melrose, believe it or not, was my grandmother's name. Aelfin's coffin was also teak, slightly smaller than mine, and open. There was no body inside, only lots of white satiny material edged with lace. Her lid was propped up against the wall. It read: Aelfin Filide Dixon. Filide is Italian for Phyllis, which is Greek for "greenery." So that figures. Not.

Our names, my father claims, are due to an article my mother read in *The Times* newspaper three weeks before my birth. The article asserted that "children with unusual names go farther in life." I always scoffed at that, but in the light of my journey to an unknown universe and back again as a ball of mist, maybe there's something in it after all. My parents, by the way, are called Bill and Sarah. I think my grandmother named my mother Sarah after being burdened herself with the name Melrose, but some people are unable to learn from the mistakes of others, they prefer to do the fouling-up themselves.

Bang! It's only the double doors at the far end of the room opening, but it makes me jump. I think I'm suffering from postexplosion, posttraumatic stress syndrome. Do you think balls of mist can sue?

A pimply young man in a dark suit wheels in a steel gurney with a body bag on it.

"There you go," he says as he brakes it up in a kind of alcove with a washbasin.

"Thanks, Alan." The boy is followed by a relaxed-looking woman in her early thirties, carrying what looks like an airline pilot's bag.

Alan goes out and clangs the doors behind him.

The woman unzips her bag and gets out a white coat and a pair of thin blue gloves.

I float a little closer, although I've got a bad feeling about the body bag. As I get nearer to the woman's head, she shivers a little and turns to look at the thermometer hanging on the wall. It reads -10 degrees. She gives it a little tap of disbelief.

"Am I making the room seem colder?" I ask, but of course she doesn't answer on account of my remark being soundless. I shout to see if this will help, but it doesn't. Bit like talking to Dad when he's reading the newspaper—zero response.

The woman puts on the white coat and the blue gloves, takes a pair of blue overshoes from a locker, and tunes the radio to Classic FM. Then she turns to the body. I'm wrong about bag, actually it's just an over-wrap of black plastic, underneath which is a white cotton shroud. The woman unwinds both of them—and, of course, it's Aelfin. I knew it would be Aelfin, but still I'm shocked. There are stitches down Aelfin's neck, the length of her torso, and others that seem to start behind her ears. She looks small and white and abused.

"Aelfin," I cry.

"Poor kid," says the woman, but she's picking up a scalpel. She's going to have a go at my sister with a scalpel.

And yes, I know it's only Aelfin's *body* that's about to be attacked, and what use is a body to anyone now, but I'm still not so happy about that knife. Aelfin just looks like she's been through enough already. More than enough: an explosion, an autopsy, the lifelong curse of a sister called Cassina.

The woman aims the scalpel at Aelfin's throat; she's going to open her up again.

"No way!" I cry and I dive toward my sister's neck; position myself, the whole droplet fist of me, over the first stitch.

I tense, at least I feel tense, although my droplets seem to remain quite unmoved. The knife descends. It slices right through me; there is no pain at all. All that happens is that my droplets reform around the knife, as though it was me holding the blade. What is this, some sort of metaphor, because I did it, because I took Aelfi to that station, got her killed?

I pull away and my droplets just reform, close up again, as though the knife has never been. I watch the stitches coming away then, one, two, three, lightly cut, down to Aelfin's breastbone.

I find I'm trembling. I don't know whether it's rage or fear or uselessness or just exhaustion. This has not been a good twenty-four hours. I think I'm finally about to lose it when I have this Positive Idea: What if what happened to me also happened to Aelfin, and actually she's all right, just holed up inside her own body, crouched in a little ball of mist like me? It would be a shame to get all twisted up about her if she's just playing dead. Playing dead would be typical of her. That's how annoying she can be. And it's not such a crazy idea. I mean, I went up beyond the known universe and came down . . . where? Close to my body, that's where. Or, more specifically, close to the remains of my body. (I'm presuming my coffin's shut because there isn't much left of me, not much that you'd want to see, anyhow.) So—suppose Aelfin was thrown up, too, only somewhere different from me, but suppose also that she had to return to Earth close to her body, what then? She could be hiding right inside her own head, just a moment away from me.

You've never seen a ball of mist move so fast. I float right round the back of Aelfin's head and pass through the skin slit. The back of Aelfin's skull has been removed and her brain is missing. What do they do in those autopsies? She died in an explosion. What else did they need to know?

"Aelfin, Aelfin," I'm calling as if I expect her just to pop up her own neck and say hi. But she doesn't, and I know immediately she's not going to because this body does not feel like Aelfin at all. It's totally empty. It feels like a violin case with no violin in it.

Then I know I'm going to cry. Which is stupid really, because I've known what I've known for over twenty-four hours now. No, much longer, because while I was floating up and down, Aelfin's obviously had time to be picked up and taken to the mortuary and be chopped up by some pathologist and brought here to the undertaker's. So my understanding of time has gone AWOL as well as everything else. Not that that matters. What matters is—Aelfin's dead.

She really is dead.

My sister.

And I'm obviously dead, too, or half-dead, anyway. And where's my mom? And I can't even cry properly. I'm made of hundreds of water droplets, but I can't do tears. I'm just floating here, feeling all crushed up inside and, Aelfin, oh,

Aelfin, why did I take you to the station? I'm so sorry, Aelfin.

Aelfin, where are you?

You know when you cry and cry until you feel all dried out? Well, after a bit that's what I feel like. And I don't want to leave Aelfin—partly because I don't want to see what the scalpel woman's doing right now—but more because that would mean a good-bye, wouldn't it? Good-bye, Aelfin. And how can you say good-bye to someone who doesn't say good-bye back?

But I've got to get out because I'm drying up, and not just because of the crying, either. To tell you the truth, I began drying the moment I arrived back on Earth, but it's not as if I haven't had other things to think about, so I've been trying to ignore it. The sensation is hard to describe, but it's as though the little drops of me are shriveling at the edges; as if I'm getting smaller, drying up from the outside in. In short, I'm evaporating. It's getting so bad now I can barely move. If I don't get out of Aelfin now, I might never be able to get out. So I force myself back through the neck slit.

Good-bye, Aelfin. Good-bye.

Silence.

Scalpel-woman is busy doing something with a long white sausage I don't really want to think about. If I had a back, I'd turn it, but I have no back, so I just hover there looking at the woman's face, concentrating on her neat nose. She sniffs a little, and I have this sudden thought which is so wacky I can't believe I'm having it: *I'd be safer in there*, I think.

Safer where exactly? In the woman's head? This has not been a day when rational thought has proved very effective, and because I'm exhausted and also because Aelfi's dead and actually I don't care too much about things right now, I go up the woman's nose. I want to apologize for the invasion of privacy, explain my position as an abandoned, abandoning, evaporating ball of mist, but I can't do much more than concentrate on the darkness of the tunnel in which I find myself and the horrifying prospect that the woman might sneeze. But she doesn't sneeze and I keep on going, around a few U-bends, along the sinuses, and into the brain.

Well, it's my first time in someone else's brain, and it's a bit of a surprise. I always imagined the brain like recently boiled spaghetti: curled, soft, wet, and basically harmless. It's certainly moist (which gives me immediate and blessed relief from the evaporation syndrome), but it also seems to be conducting electricity. Sudden and quite unpredictable sparks rip between the different sections of the brain. No, maybe not sparks, as *sparks* implies heat and light. These are more like zaps and fizzes of invisible energy. Is this what they call *synapse*? I wish I'd concentrated more in biology. At first I think, if I get hit I'll be a goner (not that that would be news in the circumstances), but guess what, it turns out I'm a conductor. Not the sort that stands on the platform of a bus or in front of an orchestra, but the sort that transmits electrical current. I fizz, I pop, and while the sensation is not exactly painful, it's not something you'd choose, either; it feels like a series of buzzing shocks, as if you were repeatedly offering yourself to a cattle prod. So I'm quite glad to see the canyon. Canyon's a bit of an exaggeration; it's a fissure, I suppose, located somewhere below what's probably the frontal lobe. Anyhow, I'm not fussy, I just squeeze myself right in there; any port in an electrical storm, as it were. It's only when I'm sheltered that I realize I can see, not just along the length of the fissure but along some further channel, right out of the woman's own eyes and to the scalpel in her hand. Maybe my fissure runs close to her optic nerve.

This is what I see: the scalpel digging into the white

sausage and, as it's drawn along its length, a sudden deflation and a huge puff of escaping air.

Phew, lucky ten years in the job have dulled your sense of smell, Jane Barnes! These words are accompanied by a flurry of electrical activity in the brain somewhere just above me. *Probably the effect of the formaldehyde. I wonder if Health and Safety have ever checked it out?* More fizzes, but Jane Barnes's jaw has not moved, no words have come out of her mouth.

Most gas I've ever seen in a child's intestine. Poor kid. And I think, simultaneously: *That'll be the cinnamon Danish,* and also: *You pig, that's my sister you're talking about,* and also: *I don't believe it, I can hear this woman thinking.*

"Hello!" I cry. "Hello, Jane Barnes, can you hear me?"

Whizz, bang, zap. *Mustn't forget the sausages for Jemima's tea. Could pick them up on the way back from the school run,* Jane Scalpel Barnes thinks.

"Hello! It's me: Cassina! I'm in your brain. Knock, knock. I'm a really interesting person." And then I say it again, quietly, by thinking, as though I might be able to communicate with her that way, thought process to thought process.

Jane Barnes drops the degassed intestine into a bucket.

"Hello, Jane?" I'm not going to think about the intestine in the bucket. What use is an intestine to my sister now?

Better get going with the embalming, Jane thinks.

So that's what it is, embalming. They've cut Aelfin up, and now they are going to try and make her look pretty. Mind you, I killed her, so it's not entirely "their" fault.

Jane bends down to start up a machine which seems to be some sort of pump. Blood comes into Aelfin's chest and is sucked away by metal pipe, to be replaced, presumably, by the pinky viscous liquid in the pump's second bottle: formaldehyde?

Got to get Jemima a new ballet skirt, thinks Jane Barnes.

And I'm just about to get cross (because Jane doesn't

seem to care, not a bit, and okay she can have her random thoughts, but can't she have some decency as well?) when Barnesie takes Aelfin's small and very white left hand and starts stroking it. Of course, she's not really stroking it, probably just massaging it to try and get the formaldehyde right to the tips of Aelfin's fingers, but it's a gentle movement, and it seems caring. As I watch, Aelfin's hand, very gradually, turns pink. It looks more normal. Jane Barnes changes arms, massages Aelfin's right hand. Then she repeats the process on Aelfin's legs, left, right. She takes Aelfin's tiny feet in her gloved hands and rubs them gently pink.

I wonder if she did ballet, Jane Barnes thinks. *Poor kid. Poor parents.*

The radio is playing "Jupiter" from Holst's *The Planets.* The one you sing in assembly as "I vow to thee my country." The one with ways of gentleness and paths of peace.

I have another useless little sob then. Actually it's more of a gulp. Sob, gulp. Pathetic really. Get a grip, Cassina. Pull yourself together.

Good-bye, Aelfin.

Jane Barnes finishes her work. She scatters some sort of powder in Aelfin's chest, and stuffs something that looks like cotton wool up Aelfin's neck. Then she pops Aelfin's breastbone back, like it was a sort of jigsaw puzzle she's done many times before. She flaps back Aelfin's skin and sews her up with mattress twine. Yes, mattress twine; that's what it says on the label anyhow. I mean, couldn't they use silk or something, something respectful?

I ease my way out of Jane Barnes's brain. I attempt to dodge the electrical impulses but get hit a number of times. Nevertheless, I feel stronger now; Jane's moisture has replenished my droplet self, and I'm resilient enough now to stay in the open air while I contemplate suicide. Yes, that's what I've decided. Death by evaporation. I've tried to be jolly since it all happened, tried to look on the bright side of things, I really have. I'm not a defeatist by nature. I can usually keep my spirits up, put a positive spin on things. But with Aelfin gone and survival apparently dependent on being up someone else's nose, what's there to live for, or be half dead for?

So I stay outside. Knives obviously can't hurt a ball of mist, but drying out, that really hurts.

Jane washes the whole of Aelfin's body with disinfectant. She does Aelfin's hair with shampoo. Aelfin has beautiful hair. It shines. Jane sprays disinfectant into Aelfin's eyes, nose, and mouth, then she wipes each eye carefully and cleans around her mouth with a paper towel. Then she puts something which might be a stitch inside Aelfin's lip. I can't say Aelfin looks natural, but she looks less bruised than she did before.

The drying at the edges has started already, just a little bit, a tingling.

From a shopping bag near her airline case, Jane extracts Aelfin's gym kit: her leotard and her little wrap-over navy sweater. She proceeds to dress my sister. The neck of the leotard is scooped and the cardigan is a V-neck, not high enough to cover the stitching. Jane tucks in a piece of white satin and arranges a pretty white lace ruff about Aelfin's neck.

Then she opens a small makeup case. Aelfin would have liked that. She matches a color to Aelfin's skin and applies a little foundation. Then she chooses a natural lip gloss and moistens Aelfin's lips. She stands back to admire her handiwork. Aelfin looks like a Snow White laid out with no Prince to come and rescue her. Jane goes back to the table and rearranges Aelfin's hair. It's not how Aelfin had it, but it looks neater.

It's nice to have Aelfin looking okay before I go. I'm quite grateful to Jane Barnes really.

Jane crosses to the door, not the clangy double doors onto the outside world but to a small door which leads to the interior of the funeral parlor.

"Keith," she calls through a glass partition.

A gray-haired man emerges from a drab office. "Right you are, Jane," he says.

He accompanies her back into the embalming room.

"Good job," he says when he sees Aelfin. "Poor little girl."

"Just a year older than Jemima," Jane says.

"Doesn't bear thinking about," says Keith.

"No," says Jane.

Together they lift Aelfin's body off the gurney and into the coffin. Jane arranges the satiny material around Aelfin so that it covers her legs and most of her torso then, once again, she adjusts Aelfin's hair.

"Better get them in then," Keith says, opening yet a third door from the embalming room. On the other side of this door is a thick red curtain. Keith draws it back to reveal a small, rectangular, cold room with a crucifix on a mantel opposite. I think it's what they call a "chapel of rest."

My coffin is resting on a cart; they wheel it through first. Then they wheel in Aelfin, only the other way around, so her feet are where my head might be. The shriveling is getting worse now, it's not just in the outer droplets anymore; it's coming inward, toward what would have been my heart.

"The father's coming in this afternoon," says Keith.

My father. My father!

"Don't envy him," Keith continues. "Always the worst, kids."

What was I thinking of? Drying out, committing suicide?

How cruel, how stupid. I make a painful way toward Jane Barnes's face. I almost creak.

"And the mother," says Jane. "Is there a mother?"

I go up Jane's nose. She sniffs again; she helps me, good good Jane Barnes.

"Yes. But I'm not sure the mother's coming," says Keith. "Not sure she can face it." He pauses. "Could you, I mean if it was your own child?"

I arrive in the fissure to moisture and a massive electrical storm. When Jane looks at Aelfin, my sister's face seems to blur, disintegrate, and suddenly there's someone else lying there. A dark-haired girl with wild, frightened eyes. The girl pleads with those eyes and then Jane shakes her head, and the picture clears. It's Aelfin again.

"Yes," says Jane. "Of course, I'd have to come."

And I'm just about to get mad at Jane again—I mean, is she saying she's a better mother than my mother?—when I hear a voice through the door to the offices: "My name's Bill Dixon. I've come to see my daughters." And of course it's my dad. I feel simultaneously moved and elated, like you do when you see the reinforcements ride in in shining armor over the horizon to relieve the beleaguered army below. My lovely, bumbly dad has come, and I can be with him, and surely he will know it's me, and everything will be all right again. Maybe he'll even be able to find Aelfin. Besides, it's wet in Jane's brain; it's miraculously, beautifully wet.

"Good God," says Keith. "He's early." He consults his watch. "Two and a quarter hours early, to be precise."

"I'd better be going," says Jane.

That's when I panic. Jane's going, but I have to stay—should I get into Keith's head or hover above the coffins and wait for Dad? The advantage of Keith's head is it will be moist, too; the disadvantage, that he might not be the one to meet Dad, bring him to the chapel—and what then? I have to hover here. I wait until the last moment, sticking with Jane's moisture right until the moment when she leaves the room, then I come out into the air.

Keith closes the heavy red curtains behind Jane, concealing the entrance. Then, from behind one of the chunky wooden candlesticks on the mantelpiece, he takes a box of matches and proceeds to light the two large, creamy church candles. He drops to his knees, switches on a discreetly placed CD player, and from a small selection of discs, chooses *Gregorian Chants.* He presses Play, and solemn music fills the room. If he stays here any longer, it would be wise to go into his brain. But he doesn't; just takes one last look around, adjusts the print of Jesus between the two candles, squints to check if it's really straight, and then leaves the room, shutting the door behind him.

I hover. I wait. I'm okay. I have enough moisture. I'm not as dry as I thought. It was just the thought of not seeing Dad that panicked me.

Dad.

Hurry up, Dad.

To calm myself I look at the picture. The print is black-and-white and composed of thousands of tiny lines of type. Underneath the print is written: "Elder Rhee of the Young Nak Church, Seoul, Korea, used 63,000 letters of St. Mark's Gospel to express his deep conviction that Christ is asking something of each of us."

I wait and wait some more. It's probably only two minutes, but time enough for me to wonder what exactly is being asked of me in this new life of mine.

3

It is Keith who returns with my father, stands and holds the door for him. My father is tall and dark-haired and, to my eyes, handsome. Today he looks small and hunched and beaten.

"Dad," I cry soundlessly.

Keith retreats quietly and for a moment Dad just stands there, staring at the coffins but not moving at all. Then a terrible noise comes out of his throat, and he throws himself over Aelfin's body, his chest over hers, his arms outstretched, as though he was clinging to the box, his cheek smashed into hers. And, hovering by the Jesus print, I can't help thinking, *That's just how the man at the station, the man covered in dust and debris, threw himself over Aelfin, the same movement, the same position exactly.*

I'm not sure how long Dad lies there. He doesn't move, and I don't move; it seems intrusive. But, of course, I'm waiting, aching for him to look to me. Eventually he pulls himself up and puts a fist under his nostrils, then he reaches out again, but not to me. He touches Aelfin's cheek, leans down for a last kiss, tiny, tender. Only then does he turn to my blank coffin; he traces a finger in the brass indentation of my name.

"Cassina," he whispers. "Oh, Cassina."

"I'm here, Dad, I'm here!" I float right up to him. "Dad, it's me, Cassina!"

He doesn't hear me; he doesn't see me. I could scream. I do scream, "Dad!"

He looks as if he needs to sit down, but there is no space to sit in this room. So he leans on my coffin; and then he raises a fist and bangs it on the coffin lid: bang, bang, bang.

I go to his face; there are tears on his cheek. I drink in the moisture (if only he knew how he was giving to me, looking after me, even now) and then he breathes in and I let myself flow into his brain. I anticipate the blessed wetness and also the intimacy: I will be able to share every one of his thoughts. I shan't care about the synapses, won't mind being fizz-cracked by my own father. At least that's what I think till I get to the fissure. Dad's brain is slightly bigger than Jane Barnes's, but it's laid out in much the same way, and I follow a similar route.

"What do you think you're playing at?" a voice says when I arrive. "Mind your particles."

At first I think it's Dad; but it doesn't sound like Dad, and it isn't accompanied by brain whizzes and pops. It's aggressive and accompanied by a sensation of being simultaneously barged and invaded, as though bits of me were being pushed about by bits of someone else.

"I said watch it!" the voice repeats.

I'm just about to retaliate when I realize it's actually me doing the barging. There is someone in Dad's fissure! Or, strictly speaking, there's another bunch of mist in the fissure, and somehow I'm mingling with it.

I shrink back. "I'm so sorry."

"You will be," the voice says. "This host is claimed."

"Host?" I inquire lamely.

"Yes." He spells it out (I'm assuming it's a he—but there's not a lot of information to go on.) "H–O–S–T, host. He's my host; I'm his para-spirit. End of story. Feel free to leave any time you want. Now would be good."

In some ways it makes sense, Dad's brain being blocked

up by some less-than-caring-sharing otherworldly being. It could account for what Mom calls his "obstinate streak," his inability to see the other person's (read Mom's) point of view sometimes. But host, para-spirit?

"Para-spirit?" I remark.

"Don't tell me," he says, "you're new on the block."

"Yes," I say.

"You don't know the rules of the game."

"Is it a game?" I ask.

He laughs, a sort of wet choke. "You die, you think you're going to heaven, and you end up as a para-spirit. Sure it's a game."

"What's a para-spirit, exactly?" I ask.

"*Para* as in 'beside' or 'beyond.' From the Greek. I don't suppose you've ever done any Greek, have you? No. Doesn't surprise me. State of our so-called civilization." He pauses. "Para-spirit, a little way beyond spirit, where spirit is soul, essence, anima. *Anima* is Latin, by the way. Don't suppose you've done any Latin, either. No, course not, silly me. Tendency nowadays to forget history, forget where we've come from. 'To know nothing of history is to remain forever a child': Cicero. What did you ask? Oh, para-spirit. You are a para-spirit—that is to say you are something, somewhere between the paranormal and a parasite, or, put another way, you are a small, dependent oddball."

"Does that go for you, too?" I retort.

He doesn't smile, because he can't, but he replies, "Probably."

"How do you know you're—we're—para-spirits?"

"I've been around a long time," he says. "You get to know people—paras—they tell you things."

It's my turn to pause, because I'm desperate to ask a question, even though I'm far from sure I really want to know the answer. But I ask anyway. "How long have you been . . . you know?"

"Half dead?" he replies. "Don't know. Can't say. You lose track of time. I know I had to move hosts four times. Two car crashes, one heart attack, and one old age. Bad luck about the car crashes. But this host's okay. Pretty docile. Doesn't think too much, or didn't used to before the explosion, so the dodging about's not too bad. And he doesn't dream that much, either, which is a blessed relief."

"You're talking about my father," I say indignantly.

"Oh, *mea culpa*. You must be Cassina, then."

Cassina, not Aelfin. "How do you know that?"

"Well, he does think about you, you know, especially since you and your sister managed to get yourselves blown up. Why did you do that to him, the poor sap? His brain's been in overdrive, and it hasn't been much fun for me."

"Well, you could move hosts again, then, couldn't you?" I say.

"Could do. But decent ones don't grow on trees. Not if you like peace and quiet—which I do. I'm hoping it will all blow over."

"Mine and Aelfin's death 'blow over'!"

"There's no need to take it personally."

"I'm not sure how else I'm supposed to take it."

"Look, you were Cassina the person, now you're Cassina the para-spirit. You need to adjust."

"How do you know I'm Cassina? How do you know I'm not Aelfin?"

He sighs. "Aelfin good, Cassina bad. Ergo, you have to be Cassina."

"Is that what Dad thinks?"

"He doesn't do a lot of thinking, I told you." My fellow para-spirit adjusts his position slightly, expands a little. "And I can see the world for myself, you know. I'm pretty sure Aelfin wouldn't have just barged in here. She'd have said please, or excuse me."

"Yeah, right. And she'd have said, 'How do you do, and

pleased to meet you, and what's your name,' all in Greek as well." I pause. "What is your name, anyway?"

"You can call me Lord Blacoe."

"You were never a lord!"

"Adjust, Cassina, adjust."

"Well, I'm just going to call you Blacoe."

"Suit yourself," he says. "You're not going to be here long."

"Who says you have priority here, anyway?"

"It's the rules, I told you."

"What rules? Who makes up the rules? Who's in charge around here, anyway?"

That shuts Blacoe up, but only for a moment. "Everyone knows the rules," he says solidly.

"Except me, that is. So why don't you help me out, tell me, give me the leg up. Not that I'm particularly good on rules, you understand."

"First come, first served on hosts," he says, "and no going into children."

"What?"

"You heard."

"Why no going into children? I am a child!"

"You were a child. Children's brains are only partially formed. You can't hurt an adult by going into their brains, half of them are brain-dead anyway. But a child, that's different. You can do damage. It's not allowed. Forbidden. *Verboten*. (*Verboten*'s German, by the way.) So it's an absolutely-no-chance, no-go area. Get it?"

"And what happens if somebody does?" I ask. "What happens if a para-spirit goes into a kid's brain, you know, by accident? What can They do to you that's worse than being a para-spirit?"

"Send you to the undiscovered country," Blacoe says darkly, "'from whose bourn no traveller returns.'"

"What?"

"Shakespeare. Don't suppose you know who he is, either."

"Course I know!"

"Right, then you know we don't want to try the kids' brain tactic in case we go somewhere worse. Better the devil you know."

"But what if you got to go somewhere better?"

"Ah—but are you prepared to take the risk, hmm?" He sounds smug. "That's why people don't go in for evaporation. Don't dare, just in case."

"Sounds like a God argument to me," I remark crossly, thinking how I nearly went in for evaporation.

Now it's his turn to say what: "What?"

"Don't eat of the tree of knowledge or else," I say. "Don't go into kids' brains or else. Don't try evaporation or else. He wouldn't like it. He's set His face against it. Well, what if He doesn't exist?"

"But what if He does?" says Blacoe complacently. "You're in a bit of a hole then, aren't you?"

"No, because He'd probably understand a little bit of enterprise. He or She. Could be a She, you know."

"You're tiring me," says Blacoe. "Isn't it going-home time yet?"

But I'm far from finished: "Do para-spirits live forever, then?" I ask.

"How should I know?"

"Well, you must have known a few," I say. "Have any suddenly disappeared; here today, gone tomorrow?"

"Yes. It happens. But they could have just moved hosts. I'm a bit of a sticker, but other people move around a lot."

"But do they—do *we*—have natural deaths? You must have wondered about that."

"We're already dead," he says comfortably.

I have never met anyone so infuriating. If he wasn't

already dead, I'd punch him to kingdom come. "And how come some people get made para-spirits and others don't?"

"What are you going on about now?"

"Well, there were loads of us in that station. And nobody came up with me. Not even Aelfin, and she was right beside me when it happened. Why was there no one else? Why just me?"

"Why do some people get born and others not?" says Blacoe.

"That's a ludicrous answer!"

"Have you got a better one?"

"Where's Aelfin?" I shout.

"In heaven probably," he says. "Or hell."

"Hell? Aelfin couldn't go to hell. Aelfin's too—" I'm about to say good and then I say, "nice. Aelfin's nice. She's lovely. I loved her."

"Heaven then. She probably got the fast one-way ticket. Didn't have to do the in-transit bit."

"Are we in transit? Is that where we're waiting to go?"

"Possibly," he says. "Although, at first, I used to wonder if we might not go the other way. Get to be alive again."

"Oh sure," I say. "Take a look at my closed coffin down there. I wouldn't bet on my body resurrecting."

"There were rumors," Blacoe says meditatively. "I did hear rumors once, that there was a way."

I can't help myself; I'm interested. "What rumors? What way?"

"Probably nothing. Probably just the triumph of para-spirit hope over para-spirit experience. Not that I really want to be human again. I think I've gone past it now, seen it, done it, grown out of it. Besides human life is so . . ." he pauses, choosing his word with care, "passionate."

"And that's a bad thing?"

"It's exhausting."

"Were you old when you died?"

"I can't remember," he says.

"I think you must have been. I think you must have been on your last legs anyhow."

"You'll calm down," he says placidly. "You'll see."

"I'll never calm down. I don't want to calm down," I say.

"Being a para-spirit and being passionate are mutually exclusive. You see there is nothing you can *do* as a para-spirit. Your host can't see you. He can't hear you. He can't feel you. You have no influence. You are powerless, Cassina."

"I don't do powerlessness."

"But you will, Cassina. You will even get used to the loneliness. After a while you will find these questions less important. You will learn to adapt. You may even have fun."

"Fun. Fun! Do you and your fellow paras go out for evaporation parties or something? Or invite a pal around for an evening in, in your host's brain?"

"Speaking for myself," says Blacoe, "no. I like the quiet life, as I've said. But there are other things to enjoy, Cassina. The journey, for one. You need to let go a bit."

"Letting go is not my thing!" I yell.

"Yes," says Blacoe. "I can see that. I'd say your chances of survival as a para-spirit are slim."

"Survival of what, for what! I'm dead, aren't I?"

"Do you think you could go now?" he says. "I think mine host is about to depart, and it could be a good time for a nap."

That's when I realize I've missed it. All of Dad's thoughts about me. Me! While Blacoe and I have been talking, Dad's brain has been fireworking, there has been a November Fifth display of love and grief, and I've been idling away the time with some jumped-up, opinionated half-life. And why? Because he speaks back, because he's the first person who's actually answered me since the explosion, and you know what? It is very dispiriting talking to yourself all the time. So yes, I enjoyed our little chat, but I've missed all Dad's innermost thoughts.

"I've missed it!" I shout. "You made me miss my dad's final good-byes!"

"I did nothing of the sort," said Blacoe. "You barged in here without so much as a say-so and have kept up a constant stream of questions ever since."

That's true, as it happens, so there's not much I can reasonably retort.

"Besides," Blacoe continues, "I can tell you what he said: *Why me, why my girls? What kind of God allows this sort of thing to happen? Why did it have to be parents' night? Why did they go to the station? Why didn't I go home? I should have been there. I could have protected them, saved them* (unlikely). *Oh, Aelfin, oh, Cassina, you don't know how much I loved you, love you.*" He takes a breath. "It's always the same, you see," he remarks. "Grief. He's still at the anger, disbelief stage. But it will pass. It always passes."

"Thanks," I say.

"Oh yes," continues Blacoe. "I forgot the threat stuff. *If I ever get my hands on the man behind this, I'll tear him limb from limb.*"

"What man?"

"The T'lanni," Blacoe says.

"A T'lanni?" I repeat.

"Yes," he says. "A religious plot. I thought you knew. I thought that's why you were going on about God."

"So it was a bomb."

"Yes. A suicide bomb."

When I don't reply to that he adds, "You were murdered, Cassina."

4

Murdered. That's nice. I probably made the local paper. Mom can put the article in the file of clippings along with Aelfin's gymnastic results: "Aelfin Dixon wins gold—again!" "Cassina Dixon gets—murdered!" Do I sound bitter? Trust me, I'm not. It's just it would have been nice to make the paper for something I'd done, rather than for something done to me. And who did it to me, anyway? And why? Of course I know about the T'lannis. The ones that belong to the Haliki sect, anyway: they blow things up; they blow up planes and buildings and railway stations, they've been doing it for years. Thing is, I've never stopped to ask why; bit of a mistake, that. Right, let's go back to basics. What exactly do I know about T'lannis in general? Scroll down to Comparative Religious Studies. Oh yes, I remember; it's the smiting lot. About three thousand years ago, God sent His bearer—the angel Ingali—to deliver His message to the people of Earth. "And Ingali smote the desert with the Word of God."

Smote—isn't that such a great word? I always wanted to use it in everyday conversation. As in: "Guess what happened in geography today, Mom? I smote Miss Frobisher." Anyway, Ingali smote the desert, and trees grew and water flowed and God said, "Make here a city to me and call it Sacrini." Only trouble was there was already a city there, or at least a few mud huts and some other people who considered the land theirs. And they've been fighting about the land pretty much ever since. That's about all I remember. Not that it explains much. I mean, what exactly has any of that got to do with a bomb in the station of my hometown?

"Why do they do it?" I ask Blacoe then.

"I thought you were going," he replies.

"Why do they blow people up? Blow themselves up? Why do they do it?"

"They don't like us."

That's Lord Blacoe for you: razor-sharp nonbrain, straight to the point.

"Why don't they like us?"

"We're not them."

"What?"

"We don't wear the right hats."

"Hats? What hats?"

"Or shoes," Blacoe says.

I'm about to say "you're joking" but stop myself. My acquaintance with Blacoe may be brief, but I don't have him down for the joking sort.

"When you were alive, Cassina," he continues patiently, "did you succumb to wearing labels?"

"Labels? You mean like designer clothes? What do you think I am, a townie?" Actually, I never had the money.

"People who wear Nike sneakers," Blacoe continues, "they're not wearing them for comfort, they're wearing them to show they belong, to identify their group. We are the Nike Sneaker People; you who don't have the sneakers are not our group. Us and Them. It's about gangs."

"I don't get it."

"Okay, I give in," he says. "It's about the walls."

"Walls?"

"That's what I said."

"What walls—exactly?"

"Take your pick. They're all pretty much the same. Hadrian's wall, built in AD 122 to separate the Romans from the Barbarians; the Great Wall of China erected by Emperor Shi Huangdi to keep the Mongol hordes at bay; the Berlin Wall. All built to keep people in. Or out. Depending on your point of view."

"Are you talking about the wall around Sacrini?"

"Oh, so they did teach you something at school after all."

"But that's a really old wall," I say. "That wall's been there for over two thousand years!"

"The old walls," says Blacoe, "they're always the best."

So I got him wrong. He does have a sense of humor after all.

"Only," Blacoe continues, "whereas the wall used to be a few mounds and the odd ditch—"

"Now it's barbed wire and concrete and gun turrets."

"Exactly."

"Exactly what? I mean, it doesn't explain anything does it?"

"Oh," says Blacoe. "Perhaps I failed to mention the little issue of God. T'lannis—the Haliki type anyway—also believe we don't worship the right god."

Might have known. "And who exactly is the right god?"

"The one they worship, of course."

"This is the twenty-first century, Blacoe!"

"History, Cassina, history. Not a lot changes. You have to understand that the genetic structure of human beings mutates at the rate of only half a percent every hundred years, so while we may have got smarter at some things, like tools (flint to microchip), our morality remains essentially tribal, Neanderthal even."

"How do you know all this stuff?"

"Thinking is something para-spirits get a lot of time to do."

"Doesn't give them the right to kill us though, does it?"

"Do you know anything about the Crusades, Cassina?"

"Not really."

"History. Excellent subject history. Much underrated."

"Well?"

"Christians went rampaging across the earth, killing people. And why do you think they did that?"

"No idea."

"It's a long story. But you could say it was because they feared for the souls of the unbelievers. They thought those poor people would go to hell if they weren't converted. And also, there was the small matter of indulgences. If you went on a Crusade, you yourself got your sins forgiven. You went straight to heaven. A good deal for people for whom heaven and hell were rather closer than they are for us today."

"And the T'lannis still believe that sort of stuff?"

"The Haliki lot appear to, yes."

"But I thought we were supposed to have tolerance. I thought we were all supposed to live in a multicultural world. I thought things had changed."

"Human nature doesn't change much. I mentioned that already—weren't you listening? Then there's the simple matter of logic. Logic used to be taught in Greek and Roman times. Not anymore, alas."

I say nothing. My Neanderthal brain has taken on this at least: Blacoe goes at his own pace.

"Thus," he continues, "if my God is the One, True, Only God and you claim *your* God is the One, True, Only God, we have a problem, don't you see?"

"You mean we can't both be right?"

"Excellent. You're getting the hang of this."

"We could just agree to differ."

"Yes," says Blacoe. "That's when human nature comes back in. And power. And this and that. And I really don't think we have time to discuss anything more, Cassina. Sorry. Good-bye. You're taking up too much space. You're making me dry. Go away."

And he's right, of course, about the moisture, anyway. I've begun to notice it, too. Dad's brain really can't support both of us. I need the wet, but so does Blacoe. My outermost drops have begun to tingle; I'm beginning to parch around the edges. But there's just one more thing I need to know; it's nagging at the edge of my Comparative Religious Studies memory bank.

"I thought we all had the same God, really, I mean us and the Muslims and the T'lannis. One God, different interpretations."

"Oh, not so stupid, after all. Though your use of the term *us* assumes you think I, too, am a Christian. Never wise to make that sort of assumption about another person."

"Or para-spirit."

"Indeed. But One God, yes, you're right in a way. Trouble is, each religion claims to have the fullest revelation of that God: Christianity in Christ, Islam through Muhammad, and the T'lannis through Ingali. And Ingali's particularly problematic, because he wasn't just a prophet, or even the son of God; T'lannis believe he was God's 'bearer'—an extension of God himself, God's direct word on that desert sand. So that has to be best, doesn't it? Now, I won't say it again: Go away."

"Okay," I say. "Okay."

But it's not okay, because Dad has left the funeral parlor and is making his way to the car with the word *home* zapping around his brain. The very notion of home makes me feel impossibly nostalgic, as if I've been away for a hundred years. But maybe it's also because home includes my mother.

"I have to go with Dad," I tell Blacoe. "I have to get

home. I'll transfer to my mom when we get there. Promise. She hasn't already got a para-spirit, has she?"

"How would I know?"

His lack of curiosity is startling. He lives in that house, doesn't he?

"Please, Blacoe?"

"Very well, but you'll have to go to the basement."

"Basement?"

"The heart department. There's a small amount of space in most heart chambers. The view isn't great, but it's safe enough."

He explains the route, which involves being inhaled into the lungs and floating along some vein toward the left ventricle. What he doesn't tell me is that getting into the lungs is a bit like trying to go down the up escalator: Every time you think you have arrived, your host takes another breath, and you get swept back up to the nose. But I decide to be positive and look on it as a para-spirit equivalent of an amusement park. I inform myself that I'm on the roller coaster and it's fun. It isn't fun, actually, not if you're the sort that prefers the scenic rides, anyway.

I hold on as best I can and concentrate on the music. There's music every time you pass over the larynx; it's a wonderful sound, like faraway wind chimes. I'm just thinking, if I ever get out of here, I might patent it, when—whoosh, Dad indulges in another mighty in-breath.

This time I hang on to the branchy things in the lungs (You think the lungs are like some empty balloons, right? Wrong. They're full of these branches, which no doubt have a fancy Latin name. Must remember to ask Blacoe. Not.), and when I say hang on, I mean hang on. Now what? I spot a passing blood sac and drop onto it. Well, into it, actually, and then I'm in some sort of slipstream. The flow is rapid, could be a whole new sport; not white-water rafting, but red-corpuscle riding.

I'm telling myself this stuff to keep my para-spirit up. What if I give Dad a heart attack? After all, I am a foreign body in his bloodstream, or a foreign ex-body anyhow. I comfort myself with Blacoe's assertions that I'm passionless and powerless and can't make any difference anyway, and finally arrive in the thundering chamber. You can see why a para-spirit would prefer the brain. The heart chamber is dark and red and thumping; it's like being inside some giant generator. It's also hot and, yes, Blacoe, you can't see out. Bit like being in the coal mines in the olden days, no doubt. History, Cassina, history. I reckon they should get Health and Safety on to this, issue all para-spirits with earmuffs, or droplet-muffs, or something to stop the incredible din. It's difficult to explain exactly how loud the noise is, but let's just say, if you're a para-spirit (and, hey—I'm not wishing that on anyone), you don't exactly "hear" noise, you experience it; you reverberate with it: you rock, baby.

I can't tell you how long I spend rocking; it's a bit like one of those tortures where they keep you awake for hours, banging tins until you lose track of whether it's today, tomorrow, or yesterday. Which may account for My Inspiration. There I am being battered and dinned, while blue blood comes in from one side of the heart (blue blood's pretty spooky, I can tell you) only to emerge, after its contact with the oxygen in the lungs, red again, and kazam, I suddenly think, is this awesome or what? This human body, this thing I no longer have, the way it works, it's so exact and so intricate and somehow beautiful, too. It's getting me wrought-up, tearful, crushed inside. The human body— what a fabulous design. Give an award to the guy who thought it up.

Uh-oh, not this again. Not—The Guy Who Thought It Up. Is that the same guy I expected to meet beyond the known universe? The guy in charge, the one who might otherwise be called God? Because somebody must have thought it up, mustn't they? I mean the human body couldn't have thought itself up, could it? Developed from some primal blob? It all seems too refined somehow, too perfect.

I'm just thinking maybe I should schedule another chat with Blacoe (Do you think he was a teacher in his previous life? I bet he was, I bet he was some crusty old classics master, Mr. Blacoe, Old Flako.) when things get worse. The pumping goes into overdrive, boom, boom, boom. Sonic stuff, from which I have to intuit that Dad is on the move. He is no longer sitting comfortably in his car, he has arrived, got out, begun to strain his heart with the effort of walking. Ergo (Do you think this Latin stuff is catching?) I have to be going, too.

I need to go with the blue blood obviously, that's the way back to the lungs. Can't go with the red, who knows where I might end up? Cassina Dixon, Marooned in Ankle. Cassina Dixon, aged thirteen, Missing in Kidney. No, check, I watched the embalming, didn't I? There's a whacking great artery that leads straight up the neck and into the brain. Skip the lung roller coaster and head for the aorta. Whoa, here we go. I spread my particles into the artery current, which is strong and very red. I flow onward and upward; I'm getting the hang of this. Maybe I could be para-spirit champion? Cassina Dixon, Artery Surfing Champion of the Year. Open that file of clippings, Mama.

I burst into the brain.

"I would have called you," says Blacoe.

"Sure." And how.

It's lovely to be able to see out again. Oh, beautiful world!

My father is going up the path to our front door. I can't tell you how wonderful our front door looks. I mean, of course, it's only an ordinary blue wood door with a brass mail box, but to me it looks like a shining gateway, the promise of everything I hold dear. Behind that door is life as I know it; or knew it, anyway. Everything and everyone I care about is behind that door. My home.

"Mr. Dixon, Mr. Dixon!" Someone's shouting from behind us. "Mr. Dixon, could we have a comment?"

Dad's pace quickens.

"Mr. Dixon." Another voice, urgent, male. "Could you tell us how you and Mrs. Dixon are coping today?"

My father turns around then. In front of us are three men with notebooks, and there are others coming with cameras. There's a flash, and at first, I think it's a camera, but then I realize it's my dad's brain. My lovely bumbly dad, who's never angry, is synapsing furious red and jagged silver. And there's noise, too, a terrible thumping. I hear it even as I cower in the fissure: It's Dad's heart, hitting his chest like a hammer.

"You . . ." begins my father. "You . . ." and then his brain explodes, but not with anger, after all; the heat in his head seems to be wet. It's tears; I think it's tears.

Oh, Dad.

He pulls around, turns his back on the men, unlocks our door and slams it shut behind him. Then he stands with his back against the wood, unable to catch his breath.

For a moment the only noise is the sound of Dad's throat, the sob-sob pant of it. The house stands around him, still and quiet. It's eerie, unnerving, and not at all like life as I knew it. In the miserable silence this stupid thought pops into my ex-brain: Was it really only Aelfin and me who made noise in this place? Then—after about a million years—Bonnie, our Labrador retriever, comes bounding down the stairs and launches herself at Dad.

He pushes her away. She goes at him again. "I said get off!" Dad yells, suddenly finding his voice. Bonnie backs away.

"Sarah?" Dad calls then. "Sarah?"

Silence. A long, long silence.

"She'd better be in," says Blacoe.

"She will be," I say. "She will be."

Then I notice something else. Our house is a mess. There are actually things on the stairs: a pair of Dad's shoes, a roll of toilet paper, several official-looking envelopes, at least six separate items—on the *stairs*. Mom never leaves stuff on the stairs. Never. And I can see into our kitchen. There are dishes—not done—in the sink, a huge pile of them, and on the counter are Bonnie's dog biscuits, opened, not put away. It makes me feel all lurchy inside; how can mess make you feel lurchy?

Dad climbs the stairs, and Bonnie follows with her head down. "Oh, grow up," says Dad, and then his brain cracks again: *They'll never grow up. Never go to college; never get married, have children of their own, grandchildren. I will never have grandchildren.*

Oh, Dad, I'm here, Dad. Can't you hear me?

"Sarah?" Dad calls again, but he doesn't make for their bedroom. He crosses the landing to Aelfin's room, pushes his way through the half-open door. My mother is lying facedown on the carpet, clutching Bug, Aelfin's limp, washed-out gray teddy bear. She doesn't move when Dad comes in.

"Sarah?"

She turns slightly then. Her face is pitiful: pinched, hollow-eyed, sunk with exhaustion.

Mom!

"It's like there was a hole," she announces to the air, "here."

She draws a line from her neck to her waist. "As though they just cut everything out and left nothing at all."

But that's not the worst thing; the worst thing is that my mother is still in her dressing gown. She's lying on the floor, in the middle of the afternoon, in her blue-quilted dressing gown; my bright, busy mother, who was always up and showered and dressed by a quarter to seven. It's as painful to look at as the slashes in Aelfin's body.

The room is untouched. The bed is neatly made. Aelfin would have done that herself—as she did every morning—the day of the bomb. Her beads hang in tidy ropes on her dressing table; her place in her novel is marked with the pressed-flower bookmark she made herself; and her toothbrush stands at salute on the edge of her tiny sink. The only thing that's missing is her gymnastics bag, which normally hangs on the back of the door.

My father makes for the window and puts his hands on the curtains. There's the immediate "poof" of a camera flash.

"God damn them," says Dad and yanks the curtain closed.

"Mom," I whisper in the half-dark. She looks so alone.

"Sometimes I hear her," Mom says.

I don't believe it! "She hears me."

"She doesn't hear you," says Blacoe.

But I'm already on my way, floating out toward my mother.

"Who?" says my father.

"Aelfin," says Mom. "She speaks to me."

Okay, Aelfin, but so what? Para-spirit communication probably takes some getting used to.

"Sarah," says my father.

She hasn't moved, is still lying on the floor. Why doesn't he go to her, lift her to him? That's what I'd want to do. I float across to her face. She puts a hand up, exactly where

I am; it passes through me, brushes hair out of her eyes.

"Mom!"

What I wouldn't give now for a body. Or just a pair of arms, that would do, something to hold her with. All that time I lumped around in my Cassina body, complaining I was too fat, too clumpy, my thighs were thick, my butt too big. I had zits. I did have zits. They were just beginning to flower, little eruptions of suppurating red and yellow. But I never once thought, how nice to have a body; how good to be able to reach out, to touch someone you love.

"Mom!"

"And I can smell her." Mom brings the teddy bear to her face, inhales. "Bug still smells of Aelfin."

"I went to see her," says Dad, still near the window.

"I don't want to hear," says Mom sharply. "Anyway, you didn't see her, see them. You just saw bodies. And I don't want to hear about bodies. I want my babies alive. I want them, Bill. I want them now."

She clutches the teddy bear tighter.

And now he comes, doesn't try to touch her, but says, "I tell you, Sarah, if I could go in their place, I would. We shouldn't be alive. Neither of us."

Then she sobs, and he does hold her. Kneels down beside her and takes her rocking body in his. And I'm between them, between their wet cheeks.

After a while Mom pulls away. "Do you think about suicide?" she asks.

There's a pause, but only a short one. "Yes," says Dad.

"I do," says Mom. "All the time. And do you know what stops me? The thought that they might come back."

And I think about what Blacoe said, how there might be a way back for para-spirits. "I'll find a way back, Mom, I will. I promise."

"That they might come back," Mom continues, "and I wouldn't be here."

"Is that why you wouldn't come to the funeral home?" Dad asks.

"Perhaps," she says. "But you went." She looks at him. "And you saw them. So you know they're not coming back." She pauses, and I feel her tremble. "They're not coming back, are they, Bill?"

Yes, Mom, I am. We are. We?

"No," my father says. "They're not coming back. Not unless you believe in miracles."

Believe in them, Mom.

A small, hopeless smile flits across her face. "Then I'm going to believe in miracles," she announces.

Yes!

"Just for a while, Bill. Just a while. Please."

That's when I go into her brain, just flow with her, arrive in the fissure, which is blissfully (blissfully) vacant. My mother, my host. I expect her brain to be full of crushing thoughts, but it's not; it's full of pictures. They come so furiously that I feel assaulted, as though I was being bombarded by twenty television sets, all tuned to different channels but none of them adjusted properly, leaving the images random, blurred.

But I am determined to make sense of the pictures, to work them out, so I concentrate. Gradually I see that all the images are coming from one section of the brain and if I come out of my fissure (and of course it hurts, but not as much as not being able to read my mother's thoughts hurts) and get closer to this part of the brain, then the picture clears. I see things I've never seen before. The strongest images, playing on all the TV screens simultaneously, are of me at the moment of my birth. Memories! Of course, that's what they are, my mother's memories: me emerging from her body, screaming; me being wrapped in a tiny sheet; me being handed back to her; her looking down at me for the very first time, her first-born child. The pictures don't have sound exactly; they have emotions so raw you feel you could wound yourself on them, even though the emotion of these memories is love, a huge flooding love as if a dam broke and the love of the whole world was pouring forth. My mother pulls my baby-self toward her, holds me as tight to her chest as she is now holding Aelfin's bear.

Me. Me, not Aelfin. And, yes, I know it's selfish and I shouldn't mention the "me" angle. But it is me. And you know what? I always thought she loved Aelfin more than me. I did. Not just because Aelfin was thinner and better at stuff, but because . . . because I just felt it. Mom prefers Aelfin; Mom and Aelfin are chips off the same block, athletic and neat and good. And I'm a huge cuckoo, big and angry and bad. And of course I never said anything. What could I have said? "You don't love me as much as Aelfin?" How would that have helped? Whatever she replied it wouldn't have been enough, it would have felt like special pleading. But here it is, lodged in my mother's brain, an outpouring of pure, blind love. And there I was in life, going around noticing only the bit of my mother that told me to tidy my room, or get a move on for breakfast.

I am coming back, Mom, just to hug you. You see if I don't.

It's at that moment that there's a huge spasm in my mother's brain. All the television sets crackle and blacken as if some alien force has interrupted transmission. The new pictures that come are of the train station, they're of blood and bodies and screaming, and all the bodies have our heads, mine and Aelfin's. Mom hears the explosion—not as loud as it was but loud enough—and she sees her daughters twist, and then our legs come off and then our arms.

"It wasn't like that, Mom!" I cry.

She tries to shake the images away, but they won't go,

they keep crowding in on her, again and again she sees the whirl of bloodied arms and bloodied legs.

"Do you think they suffered?" shouts my mother.

"No," says my father. "They would have gone immediately. They would have."

"How could He let this happen?" my mother asks. "God. How could He do it?"

"I don't know," says my father.

"Children, innocent children, what had they ever done? There can't be any purpose in that. Children. I can't believe in God anymore. I just can't."

Then she drags herself to her dressing-gowned knees, clasps her hands together.

"If you are there," she says, "then prove it, God. Bring my babies back. Please, I'm begging you. . . ." and then she begins to cry again.

And I beg that God, I beg Him and beg Him. For Mom's sake. Look at her! But God, it seems, is having the day off.

I crawl back to the fissure; but even bedded deep I feel it, rock with it, her misery. It comes in waves through her brain, not fizzing, not popping, but undulating, a surging, swelling grief. And I can do nothing, can't touch her, can't communicate with her. I am, as Blacoe said, powerless.

And I'm not sure that I can bear it.

Bonnie, who has been sitting quietly on Aelfin's rug, gets up and comes to nuzzle my mother's leg.

Did anyone say anything about not going into dogs' brains?

5

Bonnie's brain is more cramped than a human brain but also more peaceful. It's like being in one of those sensory rooms they make for the partially sighted, a haven of soft colors and glowing lights. Nuzzling close to my mother, Bonnie's brain is a pale, comforting blue; when she butts at my father's legs, it's a haze of brown and yellow. She has no thoughts exactly, or not ones I can understand, but of course she has feelings, washes of warmth, excitement, empathy. I think I could fall in love with Bonnie, she's such a sweet, caring creature. I can't imagine her having a hue for spite, for example; it's just not in her color palette.

Mind you, you probably wouldn't want to stay in a dog's brain forever, it could get dull; but right now, for me, it's like curling up in bed with my "blanky." Blanky was a piece of muslin I had as a baby. I finally sucked it into extinction, but there were days, years even, when I couldn't sleep without it. The same feeling of security comes over me as I snuggle inside Bonnie. I allow myself to doze; and it's a relief; perhaps the first time I've been able to relax since my return to Earth. Love you, Bonnie.

All that stops when Mom and Dad finally go downstairs. Bonnie makes straight for the front door and begins to bark.

"That dog needs to go out," says my father.

"Yes," says my mother, moving in the opposite direction.

"Maybe you should take her out," suggests my father. "Get dressed." His voice is tender.

"Why?" says my mother. "What's the point?"

"Please," says my father.

My mother goes upstairs in her dressing gown and, fifteen minutes later, comes down dressed. It seems like a triumph. I hear her getting Bonnie's lead; so does Bonnie. Bonnie jumps at her, her dog brain firecrackering in red and green: Bonnie barks, she bounds, she lollops.

"Shut up," says my mother, trying to get the lead on.

It's strange the view you get from a dog's brain; it's about knee level. I've never inspected my mother's knees before. They're small and shapely, with good calves beneath which end in neat feet and sensible shoes. Now Mom's got something other than death on her mind, I contemplate going back into her brain—but I resist. Going for a walk from a dog's point of view could be interesting.

"Go out the back way," says my father. "There are fewer of them there."

I guess he means the journalists.

My mother goes, with me bouncing about in the head of the over excited dog, down the path to our back gate.

A man with sturdy old-fashioned shoes scrambles out of a bush, his camera clicking and whirring. "Can you give us a quote, Mrs. Dixon?" he shouts. "I mean, losing both your children . . . ?"

My mother stops, yanks me and Bonnie to a halt. She faces the brogue man.

"You're asking about my heart," she says, "and I haven't got a heart anymore."

Then she turns her back on him and walks away. And I think how beautiful she is, how much I love her.

We head right, which means we're going to the park. Left means the canal; I always liked the canal better, but today I wouldn't trust my mother so close to a body of water, so I'm glad we're going to the park.

Is it possible to shut off one's thoughts, one's para-brain? I'm going to try; I'm going to try to lose myself inside Bonnie for a time.

She bounces—we bounce—about, inspecting tree roots and bits of old food wrappers, which is when I realize para-spirits must lack a sense of smell, which is lucky, I guess, considering some of the other stuff Bonnie pokes her nose in. At one particularly interesting scent (I'm guessing dog pee), Bonnie's brain goes purple; not a steady plain purple, but a kind of raining purple, fountains of maroon and violet. Who knows how long this display would continue but for my mother tugging her away.

By the time we get to the park, it's dusk, and there's no one in the playground except for a couple of big kids, their huge sneakered feet kicking up the mud under the swings. Mom doesn't let Bonnie off the lead until we get to the more open ground beyond.

"Go on then," says Mom finally, slipping the leash.

Immediately Bonnie's off, running, dodging, snuffling, running again. Her brain is gold. And I feel a referred happiness, and it's not because of the excitement of the brown bag Bonnie stops to put her head in or the blades of grass—tall as skyscrapers—she brushes aside, but because of her running, her bounding exhilaration. Bonnie, dog with a body; Bonnie, dog with a purpose, delirious about what might lie ahead. Just for a moment I feel part of something again.

Then I hear the scream. Only it's not really a scream, of course, more a thump and some shouts of glee, and something that might—long ago—have been a scream. And, of course, Bonnie hears it, too, and she turns toward the noise. It's coming from the Blind Garden. This small walled enclave is planted with scented flowers. A concrete path, edged with a handrail, skirts the flower beds and there is a seat where you can sit beneath a weeping willow. But it's winter now, and the summer flowering bushes are stripped bare.

I see the men immediately as we come to the garden's entrance. There are three of them. I can see the whole of the first man because he's lying flat on the ground. The other two I can only see from the knee downward. One is wearing jeans and heavy, leather, lace-up boots. The second is wearing gray combats and sneakers. Their four feet move in a blur, like a fast and vicious dance, slicing through the air. Only it's not just the air that moves. It's also the man. They are kicking him. Or stamping on him, maybe.

Bonnie's head is beige; she just stands and looks.

"What on earth do you think you're doing?" I shout, only of course I don't, at least not so that anyone could hear me. So the only noise in the Blind Garden is the thump, flump of boots on flesh and the jeaned man yelling: "T'lanni bastard! Filthy, dirty Ringer!"

The man on the ground is lying with his hands about his head to protect his skull. So they kick him in the stomach. He curls with the pain.

"Leave him alone, you brutes!" I shriek. There's no courage in this, of course, because no one can hear me. Would I be so brave if I was upright human Cassina, facing the booted men myself? Maybe not. That thought makes me feel ashamed. Bonnie puts her tail down; I can see it between her legs. She turns to go.

"No, Bonnie, no." I can't just walk away from this. They're going to kill the man. But Bonnie's walking, she can hear Mom calling her: "Bonnie, Bonnie!"

It's a spontaneous decision, and probably the wrong one, but I float out of Bonnie's head and toward the man with the leather boots. I don't expect his brain to be a cozy place, but I just can't help myself. I mean—exactly what have I got to lose?

His nostrils are flared, and he's sort of snorting, like some lathered-up horse. His skin is very pale but flushed, and his lips are drawn back from his teeth.

"Why don't you go back where you came from, you filthy pig?" He doesn't sound angry, just fired up, excited. His breathing is noisy and staccato, and comes out of his throat like a series of jerky laughs.

It seems contemptible, complicitous even, to go up his nose, but I do it. Of course, his brain is fizz-cracking wildly. I concentrate my drops to make myself as small as possible and head straight for the fissure.

"What the hell do you think you're doing?" a voice says and then adds, "Yeah! Get him, Mac! Slam him!"

There's the sound of another heavy body blow.

"Yeah!" the voice exclaims. "And give 'im one for me, and all!"

The fissure, it seems, is occupied.

"I'm not sure that's entirely appropriate," I hear myself say. I sound high and trembly and a bit like my mother in her principled-teacher mode.

"Aw, shut it," he replies. "And get out of my view. In fact, get out of my host. Geddit?" He laughs. "Go, Mac, go! Haven't had so much fun since I was in the bleachers. Only we had bottles. And knives. And they fought back. This little pansy's just lying on the ground, taking it."

"Fun?" I say. "Pansy?"

"Get lost," he says and he barges me, pushing me out of the fissure far enough to be hit by a sequence of dagger synapses energizing across Mac the Thug's brain. I'm in the brain space long enough to register pain (which is small, I imagine, compared with what the man on the ground must be going through) and to note that, in some ways, Mac's brain has more in common with Bonnie's than a human being's, which is to say he doesn't seem to be having any thoughts as such, just colors, or one color anyway: an explosive fountain of blood red.

"What did the guy on the ground ever do to him?" I ask.

"The Ringer?" Mac's para-spirit replies. "What they always do, come over here, uninvited, set up their Holy Desert Word places. Holy brainwash places! Plot stuff. Bomb people. Kill them. Didn't you hear about the station bomb?"

"Yeah, I heard. I died in that bomb."

"There you are then. They did it. The Ringers."

"Yes, but not *that* Ringer—er, T'lanni—not that one lying there." Talk about taking the moral high ground; I mean what exactly have I to thank T'lannis for right now? They murdered me, right? But Mom always said you can't generalize about people. She said, if we learned anything from 9/11 it had to be that hundreds of thousands of Muslims all over the world didn't support the violence, don't support Al Qaeda. So how can we blame this T'lanni for what some Haliki madman did in his name at the station?

"What if I'd got mown down by a blue Fiat instead?" I contend, "That wouldn't mean that all blue Fiats are killing machines, would it?"

"Good as," says Mac's para-spirit. "That's what I'm saying. They're all the same, Ringers. All as bad as each other."

"Rubbish." I'm probably also taking the high ground because otherwise (*pace* my friend Blacoe), what else can I do? Lend my mist to the guy on the ground? Start from where you are, do what you can, even if it doesn't seem much; that's what I've always been taught.

"I mean," Mac's para-spirit continues, "that one on the ground might not have planted the bomb, but he'd have had a pint on the one that did, trust me. Cheers, mate, good job."

"Some of my best friends are T'lannis," I say. This isn't, strictly speaking, true. In fact, it isn't true at all. Of course, there are T'lannis in my school, but I can't say I know any of them very well, except Yvanmi, and we only meet at basketball. The others I only really notice when they're gone, and they do go; they're allowed to stay at home for religious festivals. Now I'm aware that telling lies is wrong, but I'm doing it for the greater good here, aren't I? I mean I'm trying to explain to Mac's para that some people like T'lannis, that they don't have to be the enemy. Boy, am I getting top marks in high-mindedness.

"Ringer-lover," he says or rather he spits. His droplets actually spit. Then he adds: "No—no, don't tell me, you were a Ringer yourself! That's it, isn't it? In life you were a Ringer. Yeuch. How revolting. A Ringer in my host! Get out—now!"

"I wasn't a Ring—T'lanni!"

"You were!"

"I wasn't!" My denials sound hot—and also false.

"Filthy Ringer!"

"I'm not a Ringer!" Why do I feel so angry? Because it's not true? But I just finished saying that lies don't matter. My lies anyway, my nice high-minded lies. So that can't be it, not the whole it anyway. So maybe it's actually something more shameful, perhaps I don't actually want to be thought of as a T'lanni? But I'm not a T'lanni, I'm Cassina.

"I'm Cassina," I shout.

"Yeah, yeah."

"Cassina Dixon. Is that a Ringer name? I'm a Christian!" A Christian? Do you hear that? Cassina Dixon is a Christian. A little while ago she didn't know if she believed in God, and now she's a full-fledged, signed-up member of the

Jesus clan. I'm not one of those, I'm one of these. I'm doing exactly what Blacoe was talking about, saying I wear this hat not that hat. Defining myself against the T'lannis.

He gives me a vicious little barge. "Yeah, you're Cassina Dixon, and I'm the Queen of Sheba. Oh, great hit, Mac!"

"What is your name, anyway?"

"Flynn. Not that it's any of your business."

"Well, Flynn, what if Mac kills that man?"

"Then he'll be dead, won't he? Now get out of here, Cassina Dixon, before I shove you out."

But I stand my ground (read: continue to droplet his fissure) because I haven't exactly achieved anything yet, have I? I mean, have I stopped Mac putting the boot in? No. Has my attempt to defend T'lannis—well, this one anyway—led to a change in thinking by my fellow para-spirit? No. Do you think this is the problem with words, that they don't actually get you anywhere? They're always saying at school how important words are, how you must talk things through, brains not brawn. But talking things through depends on having someone on the other end prepared to listen. And I guess that counts out Mac and Flynn.

"I . . ." I begin.

"Get out," he shouts. "Now."

I get out. If I had hands I'd throttle him. If I had feet, I'd undoubtedly kick him. But I just have the mist, so I get out.

That's when I see it, the body of the man on the ground, the way he's lying, or sprawled, the pattern that his arms and legs are making, which is the identical pattern that the man who flung himself across Aelfin made, the dusty, debris man at the station. I see it because he's still now, the assault has stopped. Mac pushes the steel cap of one of his boots beneath the inert fingers of the man's right hand. He waggles his foot, then pulls it away sharply. The man's hand flops to earth.

"Job done," he says. And he and his buddy walk away.

I hover closer to the man, a sick feeling of recognition spreading through me. No—the dark hair, the slight body, the tan skin—what's so distinguishing about that? Hundreds of thousands of Mediterranean and Near East people share these characteristics. I could be wrong. I hope I'm wrong. I concentrate on the three rings on the middle finger of his left hand, the emblem of the T'lanni religion, one gold and two silver. It strikes me then I don't know what these rings stand for, any more than I know why Rastafarians wear dreadlocks or those Indian kids tie their hair up in little white hankies. I've never asked. Did the station man have rings? How would I have seen? He was covered in dirt. The man's clothes, which look like poor hand-me-downs, something you might pick up at the Salvation Army, tell me nothing. In the station, except for the dirt, he was all but naked.

There is only one way to be sure. The man's face is turned to the ground, but I am a slim mist and I can get between his features and the earth. I only saw his face for perhaps one second, the moment before he flung himself across Aelfin, but it was a slow-motion moment and not one I'm likely to forget. I squeeze into the gap.

It is him. The man who wanted to protect Aelfin.

And, of course, I know at once I'm going to go into him. He is breathing, very shallowly, but he is breathing. I make my way painfully slowly, as if I might be disturbing him, to his brain. His brain is quiet and that surprises me, not because I expected much fizz-cracking (in fact I feared I might find no activity here at all); no, the surprise is that his brain seems not just quiet, but calm, as though he is at peace. I slide into the fissure; it seems only courteous, but it's too quiet here, almost eerie.

"Are you okay?" I ask. That's a useful question as you can see. Especially as he couldn't hear me even if he was brand spanking wide-awake.

I come out of the fissure—I mean, what's there to avoid? I take a little tour of his frontal lobes. Is it calmness or blankness? Or is he just asleep, or concussed? He could be concussed, I suppose. He should be concussed, with the beating he's taken. Is this what unconsciousness looks like from the inside? Perhaps, but something still doesn't seem right. I can't get over this feeling of calmness, so calm it's almost unnatural.

That's when he has his first flash. It zips across his brain from the same general area that my mother's memories came from: it's a hard, hot zap and it's a series of numbers, *8, 08807, 81, 9440*. It's definitely a thought because it comes in his voice, or what I imagine must be his voice, a gentle but slightly panicked tone.

"Don't worry," I say to him helpfully. "You're going to be all right."

8807814944, 08807, 944, 08807499440, his brain replies.

Maybe he's not going to be all right; maybe he's a mathematician.

The number sequences come with such urgency and ferocity that I hightail it back to the fissure. Then I have another idea: why not pay a visit to his heart? If his heart's okay, maybe I can stop the Florence Nightingale act.

Because his breathing is so shallow, it's quite easy to get into his lungs; it's like riding a soft, warm air current. A thermal, I think birds call them. I find my little blood sac and hitch a lift to the left ventricle. I feel quite pleased with myself; I'm getting to know my way around. I arrive at the heart chamber. It's dark, and red, but it is not thumping. There's a beat, of course, but it's not emphatic; it's slow, regular, calm, as if it was conserving its own energy, like the heart of a creature in hibernation. Does the heart of an animal slow in hibernation? I don't know the answer to that, wasn't alive long enough to find out, but the idea gives me some comfort. I think the man is all right, I think his body has just temporarily shut down. I decide his calmness and his quiet, steady heartbeat are okay, more than okay, they are things of joy. Hallelujah, my man lives.

Hallelujah? Is that God creeping back in again? I'm grateful to God? Which god is that, mine or the T'lanni's? The T'lanni's god has all but got his man's head kicked in. Well, maybe not his god, per se (look at my Latin, Blacoe), but the conflict between his god and mine. Why should my god mind that his god exists, or vice versa? I mean, I can see why we mere mortals would want to have the top god—same reason we like to win things at the Olympics: everyone wants to be the best, get the gold medal, that's just Human Nature, as my friend Blacoe would say. But God, him or herself? Surely God has to be above such things. Not much use being God if your morals are no better than your mortals' morals. What's the name of the T'lanni god? J'lal, that's it, I think. Well, I think J'lal and my god and Allah, I think they're all up there Having a Laugh. All three of them, or all one of them. Ho ho ho, look at those poor saps down there fighting over Moi, shame I gave them free will. Here's another problem, I keep saying "my" god when I haven't really resolved this issue; I mean is he or isn't he my god? Do I or don't I believe in Him? Got to make some time to think about that. Meanwhile, He has to be Mac's god, or why would Mac want to stamp on the T'lanni? Which makes my god the god of thugs or else Mac a man with misplaced faith. I'm getting confused. Maybe it's because there's someone in the outside world yelling "Bister."

"Bister. Bister!" It's a woman's voice, and she sounds agitated. "Bister!"

I take a swift ride up the aorta and back into my friend's

brain. Because his face is pretty much squashed to the ground, I can only see about two inches off the ground. In the grass are four small shaggy white paws and a piece of wagging tail.

"Bister!" shrieks the woman again and then, "Oh, sweet Lord."

And you know what? I hope her lord is the same as the T'lanni's lord.

"Are you okay?" she asks.

My man doesn't reply.

The woman crouches down then and I see some neutral stockings and some far-from-sensible-shoes—sandals, in fact, and it's December. A hand comes down towards the man's face. She touches his cheek.

"I'm Mrs. Laney. Martha. Can you hear me?"

My man says nothing.

"What's happened? Can you tell me what's happened?"

He can't.

She feels in his neck, presumably for a pulse. The dog's nose comes for a sniff. "Get away, Bister." His paws retreat obediently. Gently Mrs. Laney rolls the man onto his back. I get to see the sky and also Mrs. Laney's face. She's a small woman about my mother's age, her blond hair flapping around her face, her blue eyes behind over-large glasses. She looks anxious and determined.

"What's your name?"

"88078149440," he replies.

"Praise God!" says Martha Laney. She kneels beside him, lifting his head into her lap. "Tell me your name," she repeats.

"08807—"

"Not number, name. Do you know who you are? Where you are? What happened?"

He looks up at her and, for the first time, more than one

part of his brain begins to fire. I wait for some thought, some answer, but the bolts are not passing from one section of the brain to another, they're colliding, exploding into each other. He puts his hand to his head.

"Are you hurt?" Mrs. Laney asks. "Does your head hurt?"

He shakes a no.

Does this mean he's really hurt, not even to know he's hurt, after all he's been through?

He pulls himself into a rough upright position, shies away from the skirt in which he finds himself, as though embarrassed. But his body moves easily. He really does not seem to be in pain.

"Ahim," he says.

"Ahim," Mrs. Laney repeats. "Is that your name, Ahim?"

"Ahim?" he asks himself.

"What happened, Ahim?"

He shrugs.

"Where do you live, is there anyone I can call?"

He shrugs again. "Thank you," he says.

"I think you ought to go to the hospital," Mrs. Laney says. But she doesn't say, "Look at those terrible bruises on your face" or "Can I mop up the blood?" and that's when I realize that even when I floated close to his face, just after the attack, I saw no injuries.

His brain has stopped fizzing so violently, there are fewer synapses, and they are more directed. They connect. He has his first thought: *I'm all right,* he thinks. He lifts up his hands in front of his face, just as he did at the station, rotates his palms, checks his fingers. *Again, I'm all right.* And I feel myself shiver, as though it's cold, but, of course, it is not cold. Maybe it's his wonderment—his fear—passing through me. It's only a moment before his mind blanks again; the same eerie calm I felt in him when he was lying, apparently concussed, settles about him once more.

"I'll drive you to the hospital," Mrs. Laney says. "My car's just outside the park."

"No," he says. "Thank you." *Chosen*, says a voice in the cathedral space of his brain. It's not his own voice, the voice of numbers and being all right, it's a woman's voice, clear and sweet.

"Then home. Let me drive you home. You've obviously had a collapse, a shock. Something. Is there anyone at home to care for you?"

Her use of the word *home* detonates his brain again. His memory section explodes, volcanoing images. But there is nothing to see. The images are like shards of glass, sharp and painful and broken apart.

"Home," he repeats with difficulty.

"Do you have a home?" she asks. "Do you remember the address?"

He says nothing. The jagged images in his brain will not make pictures.

She looks at his clothes. "Are you homeless, Ahim?"

"Yes," he says then. His brain flashes hot, the smashed glass images seem to melt into each other. "Yes," he repeats. "I think I'm homeless."

"Then you must come and stay with us," says Mrs. Martha Laney.

6

If Mrs. Laney is going home, then so am I. I look for Bonnie. But of course Bonnie isn't there. What did I expect, that she'd wait around for me like some sort of spirit taxi service?

I've blown it, haven't I? Just one day out in the para-spirit world, and I've blown it. I have no choice but to head—in the brain of a total stranger—toward the car of another total stranger. Why couldn't I keep my droplets to myself, why did I have to intervene? If you call doing absolutely nothing for anyone "intervening"? Looks like Blacoe was right. I'm no good at this para-spirit business.

I wail on like this until we get to the edge of the park; and then I think, no, Ahim's not a "total" stranger. He belongs in my history, was there on the day I died, felt something for Aelfin. I mean friendship has to start some-where, right? Besides, Ahim's a T'lanni, and I now have a more than passing interest in discovering how the T'lanni mind works. Good. That'll make two pressing jobs for me: finding a way back to life and interrogating the T'lanni mind. That should keep my mind off how much I want my mom.

And I also want Dad and Bonnie and Blanky. But mostly Mom. How come you never really quite grow out of wanting your mom? Does my mom sometimes want her mom, my gran? I wonder. I bet she does, especially now. I bet that's partly why she sits clutching Aelfin's teddy bear so tightly. She's being a little girl again, she's feeling small.

"Mom," I cry.

"*88078*," says Ahim's brain.

I retreat farther into the fissure. When you're a human being, you can block your ears because you've only got two of them. But you can't block your droplets, first because you've got nothing to block them with and secondly because there are too many of them. So I hear all the numbers all the way to Mrs. Laney's house.

"Here we are," she says, parking in front of a five-story apartment building. There's an elevator but Mrs. Laney suggests walking to the fourth floor. Bister, who turns out to be a small white terrier, scampers gleefully, his nails making a clipping sound on the concrete.

Mrs. Laney's front door is gray and flat, and doesn't have a mail box. She puts her key into the lock. "Welcome home," she says to Ahim.

Home. If only.

The apartment has a tiny entrance area and then you're in the living room. It's a comfortable, slightly worn-out space with two red sofas and an alcove with a dining table in it. On one of the sofas sits an elderly woman, wearing a navy blue suit and a great deal of face powder. Next to her is a thin child in butterfly pajamas who looks about seven.

"This is my aunt," says Mrs. Laney brightly. "Aunt Lou. Aunt Lou, meet Ahim. And this is my daughter, Mary."

"Oh lor'," says Aunt Lou.

The child stares at Ahim. "Is he going to be staying in my room?" she asks. There's a flat, wide-eyed innocence about her face.

"No, no," says Mrs. Laney. "I'll make him up a bed on

the sofa." She turns to Ahim. "Only we did have another guest—"

"Guest!" snorts Aunt Lou.

"Who did take over for a bit," continues Mrs. Laney. "But I'm sure you'll find it very comfortable here. We'll make Ahim very welcome, won't we, Mary?"

"Will he steal the silver?" asks Mary.

"We don't have any silver left to steal," says Aunt Lou, flatly.

"Don't mind them," says Mrs. Laney quickly. And then: "Mary, I think it's your bedtime." She looks at her watch. "Yes, it is. I'll make your bedtime milk. Ahim, do sit down, please. And can I offer you a sandwich? Maybe you didn't have dinner?"

"Thank you," says Ahim, sitting. "That would be kind."

Mrs. Laney disappears into the kitchen.

Bister jumps up onto the sofa and lays his head in Mary's lap. There's a silence.

I'd like to tell you that Ahim's brain is full of interesting and interested thoughts about his new surroundings. But it isn't. His brain is in quiet mode, except, of course, for the odd whizzing number. And I'm just thinking the T'lanni mind may prove to be impenetrable when the word *chosen* suddenly fills his lobal space. *You're chosen.* The words come like someone shouting in a church; they feel too loud, unseemly, but the voice is a woman's: sweet and clear. Ahim's head rocks; he feels the eyes of the women on him.

"I'm sorry," he manages.

"Sorry?" questions Aunt Lou.

"Sorry," says Ahim, shaking his head, ". . . if . . . if I intrude."

"Oh, don't mind us," says Aunt Lou. "Martha Laney's home for distressed Godfolk. We're used to it."

He has shaken the word away. But I can still hear it, like

an echo: *Chosen. Chosen,* and with it a small, bunched-up feeling of misery. And then I feel pretty bad just sitting around in Ahim's brain, doing precisely nothing. I mean, surely I can do something to help this man? Pressing job three: Help Your Fellow Man.

"Are you going to stay weeks?" asks Mary.

"No," says Ahim. "I don't think so."

There's another silence, and then Aunt Lou says, "Do you like soccer?"

There's zero reaction for soccer in Ahim's brain. Whatever he's been chosen for, it certainly isn't soccer.

"I'm going to watch it later," says Aunt Lou.

No reaction.

Her pink lips bunch up, a little powder falls off her face. "It's Arsenal," she says.

"Ah," says Ahim.

"Against Man U."

"Man you?" he repeats politely.

"Manchester United," says Aunt Lou. "The enemy."

"Yes," says Ahim.

Thankfully Mrs. Laney returns. She's carrying a tray on which there is a steaming glass of milk and a generous sandwich cut into triangles, the ham bursting out of the bread. I have a sensation of hunger, which I imagine is like the feeling you get in an amputated limb because I don't have a mouth anymore, or a stomach, so how can I have hunger? Concentrate on something else, Cassina. Take your mind off those lovely sandwiches, concentrate on your host, his mathematical state of chosen-ness. Perhaps you could help him go a stage further, discover who exactly he is? That would be something for the scrapbook: "Cassina Dixon aids T'lanni to Discover Self."

"I hope you don't mind eating on your knees," says Mrs. Laney, handing Ahim the plate.

"No, no, thank you."

"Be careful of the milk," Mrs. Laney warns Mary. "It's hot."

Mary blows on the milk, and Ahim looks at the sandwich.

There's another pause.

"I hope ham's all right," says Mrs. Laney. "Do you like ham, Ahim?"

"I don't think so," says Mary, mimicking.

"He's a T'lanni, isn't he?" says Aunt Lou. "T'lannis don't eat meat."

"Oh my Lord," says Mrs. Laney, snatching up the plate. "I'm so very sorry, Ahim. Please forgive me. Cheese, would cheese do?"

"I don't want to be any trouble," says Ahim.

"You know," Mrs. Laney continues with a high, fluty laugh, "I once had a Jewish gentleman here and we were having pork for supper and I said, never mind, I'll make you a bacon sandwich instead!"

"Why don't you eat meat?" Mary asks.

"The killing of animals is hateful to God," intones Ahim.

"Unlike the killing of people," remarks Aunt Lou.

"Aunt Lou, *please!*" exclaims Mrs. Laney.

That's when the numbers in Ahim's brain are blasted aside by a huge electric spasm in his memory lobes, and this gives me my Big Idea. It's all just electricity, isn't it? And I'm a conductor, aren't I? I've learned that much by being synapsed. So maybe I could do it, maybe I could help him connect with himself?

Ahim leans forward, and his words come very fast: "The T'lanni religion is one of peace. The Holy Desert Words say it is the duty of every T'lanni to make his peace with his god and with his fellow man. *Antab batak!*"

"Quite," says Mrs. Laney. "Exactly. Well said. Now I'm going to make that sandwich."

"*Antab batak?*" repeats Mary.

"Praise to the Holy One," translates Mrs. Laney. "Now, off to bed with you."

Even from inside the fissure, I can see the two glowing points at opposite ends of Ahim's memory lobes. These points look active, as though they are just waiting for something—or someone—to bridge them. Me! Cassina Dixon, the Incredible Connection.

"Aunt Lou," says Mrs. Laney, "perhaps you'd be good enough to help Mary brush her teeth tonight?"

"I haven't finished my milk," says Mary.

"Well, hurry up then," says Mrs. Laney, and she makes determinedly for the kitchen. I make for the memory lobes.

We all hear the noise of the ham sandwich going into the trash.

Aunt Lou stands up. "Come on, Mary," she says. "Say good-night to Ahim."

"Good-night, Ahim," says Mary.

I make myself into a thin chain of droplets. As I get nearer the glowing points, I see there are about five of them. This gives me pause—how do I know which should be connected to which? What if I connect him all wrong, wire his memory of his mom with that of a sausage, for instance? Not good. And what if it hurts? Hurts me, that is? And it will hurt, though probably not any more than being hit by an ordinary synapse. Do you think I'm chickening out?

"*Salullah*, Mary," says Ahim, holding up his left hand in a kind of salute.

Mary giggles. "I like your rings," she says. "Do you like my ring?" She holds out her hand to show him the face of Mickey Mouse.

"Is that what you believe in?" he asks. "Mickey Mouse?"

She draws back her hand.

I, on the other hand, choose two glow-points and connect.

The charge volts through the chain of me; the pain is intense. I fizzle, I crack, and I want to let go. But I can't let go, I'm attached, stuck, strung out like some cartoon version of myself, all points and statics, and it hurt, hurt, hurts. "Lemme go," I yell.

That's when Ahim's frontal lobe illumines and, as it does, the back memory lobes, to which I am attached, are plunged into darkness. I am released—or rather thrown violently—from the glow-points. I land on some beautiful wet spongy gray matter. Brain cells. Bliss—bliss for my singed droplets.

Ahim begins to chant and from my exhausted, prone position, I watch him hold up his left hand and move his right fingers with a kind of ritual precision. "My rings are my belief. I believe in J'lal, the One, Holy, Only, God." He taps the gold ring nearest his knuckle. "I believe in Ingali, His Angel and His Truth, who smote the desert with the Word of God." He taps the middle ring. "And I believe in the destiny of my own deeds, that whatsoever I do well in this life will do well for me in the afterlife and whatsoever I do ill will go ill for me in the afterlife." He taps the final, silver ring.

"Are you a robot?" asks Mary.

I'm beginning to like Mary. But no, Ahim's definitely not a robot. He's a human being, one I'm clearly not allowed to play with, just like Blacoe said. No interfering, no intervening, you are powerless, Cassina, you can't make Ahim fire just because you want to. That would be playing God, I suppose. Oh-oh, God again. Must have a think about God, I promise myself. But not now. Now it's enough just to lie here on the nice spongy stuff, exhausted.

"Bed," says Aunt Lou.

"Why are there two silver rings and one gold?" asks Mary.

"Two gold," corrects Ahim. "Yellow gold for my god. White gold for the angel Ingali, both of whom stand forever and remain unblemished forever. Like the gold. But my deeds, they may tarnish. The silver ring, which represents my deeds, may need polishing. It's to keep me aware, mindful of my duties."

"Bed," says Aunt Lou.

You know what I'd like to do now? Go into Mary. I feel a little burned and—frankly—embarrassed in here. Sorry, Ahim. You're on your own with your identity crisis. Scrap pressing job three. As for me, I think I need to hole up somewhere normal for a time. Gather my troubled spirits, take a rest. I float out of Ahim's nose, expecting pain, but there is no pain. It appears that I'm not really singed after all—or maybe paras just heal very fast? I don't know, but I don't feel too bad anyhow, and I don't look brown. I still look pretty transparent, pretty misty which, for me, I guess is about as normal as it gets.

I hover very close to Mary's face. She has mousy-colored hair to just below her shoulders and large, brown, well-spaced eyes. Her nose is small and snub, and she has a slightly pointed chin. The first of my droplets are very close to her left nostril, but I'm hesitating. I know I'm not allowed to go inside. Maybe that's part of the attraction. You know those signs Keep off the grass? Well, they always make me want to go on the grass, stamp on it even. I don't really believe I could hurt her by going into her brain, but of course I can't be sure. Rationality tells me this: Her brain is not, as Blacoe said, only "partially formed," it's fully formed, just not grown to its full size yet. So where's the harm? As I've just discovered to my cost, your host might be able to zap you; but you don't seem able to zap him, so I can't see in what way you could possibly damage a child. And yet I'm still hesitating.

"Bed!" shrieks Aunt Lou.

Perhaps I'll take a tour of Aunt Lou instead. I change my hover position. Aunt Lou looks like she would once have had sharp features, high cheekbones, a chiseled jaw, an aquiline nose. But her flesh now sags about her skull. She looks dragged down by gravity and face powder. I slip up her right nostril that is full of hairs, not the light, fine, delicate sort which act as the nose's cleaning system, but large spiky hairs. I can feel them pierce through my droplets.

I don't know how old Aunt Lou is, possibly in her seventies, but hers is definitely the oldest brain I've been in. It's moist, of course, but not that moist. In fact there's a thin, dried-up texture to the surface of her brain, and the fissure is narrowed like it's begun to silt up. Just what the recovering para-spirit needs. Not.

He could be an ax-murderer, Aunt Lou thinks.

So much for normal. I presume this synapse (which is accompanied by a very small whizz) refers to Ahim as he seems the only male in the household. Which makes me think, simultaneously: Where's Mary's father? And isn't it good to be back in a brain which doesn't do numbers? Besides, Ahim could be an ax-murderer. It's a point of view.

"Oh, for goodness' sake," Mrs. Laney says, returning with the cheese sandwich. "You two haven't got very far, have you? And you know it's my Samaritans evening tonight, Lou." Mrs. Laney hustles Mary away.

Aunt Lou sits down. *Alone with ax-murderer*, she thinks. She stands up, nods at Ahim, and retreats to the kitchen. She fills a kettle with water and sets it on the stove. She makes Earl Grey tea with real tea leaves which she clips inside a stainless-steel strainer.

In her head there is a small synapse of a silver tea strainer. The picture is accompanied by an emotion that feels something like a sigh. The image gets bigger. It's a beautiful one-cup tea strainer with elegant silver whirls in the handle and its own hallmarked silver stand. *Stolen*, thinks Aunt Lou. *My grandma's.*

Mrs. Laney comes bustling in with her coat in her hand.

"Did you offer Ahim a cup?" she asks.

"No," says Aunt Lou. "He's an ax-murderer."

"Don't be silly, Aunt Lou."

"You can't go out and leave us here."

"I have to. You know I do," Mrs. Laney says. "Friday's one of the busiest nights for suicides. The phone lines have to be manned at all times. A delay in phone response time could cost a life."

"What if it costs you a life to go out? Two lives. What if you come home and find us with axes through our heads?"

"Lou, the apartment doesn't even have one ax, let alone two." Mrs. Laney grabs her car keys. "Now be nice to him." She pulls on her coat. "I've left the bedding out, so you don't have to do anything."

Aunt Lou stirs her tea.

For a moment I contemplate hitching a lift in Mrs. Laney's brain and spending the evening listening to the tales of the suicides. But it's too close to the bone; just the word *suicide* reminds me of Mom in the blue dressing gown and all the unbearable stuff I'm trying to shut out. So I decide to stay home.

Home.

"Besides," says Mrs. Laney to Aunt Lou, "you've got Bister."

"Oh, Bister," says Aunt Lou. "That rottweiler."

"Look," says Mrs. Laney, "you have to trust people. If nobody trusts anyone else, we're all finished."

Aunt Lou washes the stainless-steel tea strainer noisily under the tap. "Like you trusted Bill," she remarks.

"He probably needed that stupid silver strainer more than you!" explodes Mrs. Laney.

"Bill didn't drink tea," Aunt Lou says. "He only drank whiskey."

"'The Lord is with me,'" quotes Mrs. Laney. "'I will not be afraid. What can man do to me?' Psalm one hundred eighteen."

"Well, the Lord might well be with you," says Aunt Lou, "but that doesn't mean He's necessarily with me. Or Mary," she adds pointedly.

"Do you really believe I'd go out if I thought Mary—or even you—were in danger?"

"Yes," says Aunt Lou.

"That's just rubbish, Lou. How many people—how many strangers—have we taken in over the years? Eight? Ten? And, with the minor exception of Bill and his perfectly understandable misdemeanor—"

Aunt Lou snorts.

"—have they been dangerous? No, they have not. Occasionally they've pinched a drink or been a bit rowdy—but that's all. All, Aunt Lou. Mostly they've been grateful, charming even. They've *given* to us."

"Always a first time," says Aunt Lou. "Anyway, I don't trust him."

"'"Have faith in God," Jesus answered. "I tell you the truth, if anyone says to the mountain—"'"

"Go chuck yourself in the sea," interrupts Aunt Lou. "It will be done."

"Exactly," says Mrs. Laney. "Mark, chapter eleven, verse twenty-two. But only if you pray. I pray all the time. For Mary—and for you, Aunt Lou."

"Right," says Aunt Lou.

"So, I'll see you in the morning." Mrs. Laney begins to exit and then turns around again. "Besides," she adds, "Ahim is a religious man himself."

"That's a comfort," replies Aunt Lou.

Mrs. Laney goes through into the living room. "Bye, Ahim," she says. "Don't wait up. I'll come in very quietly."

Aunt Lou remains in the kitchen, drinking her tea standing up by the counter. *One ax-murderer,* flashes her brain, *and one soft in the head. Only me standing between Mary and the Hordes of Hell.* When she's finished the tea, she washes and dries her cup, washes and dries the saucer and puts them both away. Then she goes along the corridor to a door which is wedged open with a white fluffy duck-billed platypus with a bright orange beak. She looks inside. It's Mary's room, and Mary is lying in bed on her back, her arms flung wide.

Poor fatherless child. Then some pictures start in her brain and of course I want to see, so I creep out of the fissure. But I find it's actually not pictures plural; it's just one picture, brightly colored and very exact, as if Aunt Lou has logged the most minute details of the scene. It's a picture of a sandy-haired man, with precisely the same elfin features as Mary, standing on the concrete staircase outside the apartment with a suitcase in each hand. You can see the brass clasps, and how tightly he's holding the handles.

"You love God more than me," he says in a tired, flat way, "that's all there is to it." Then he turns away and walks down the stairs, deliberately bumping the suitcases. Bump, bump, bump, the two suitcases not quite in time with each other. Mrs. Laney shuts the apartment door, but not before there's a terrible wail from inside. Mary. "Dad!" she shouts, but he doesn't turn around.

Aunt Lou remains standing in Mary's doorway a moment longer. Then the picture closes off, and she sighs. Back in my fissure I feel her sigh like a deflation. Aunt Lou returns to the living room.

"Do you mind?" she says to Ahim and switches on the television. She depresses the play button. The blare of crowds and game music comes on. "It's not live," she says. "Martha won't have the sports channels. My friend Ted records it for me. Every week."

It's strange to see Ahim from the outside again. He looks small and uncomfortable and has his hands interlocked in his lap. He does not look like an ax-murderer. I don't know how old he is, maybe twenty-five, twenty-six; but he looks like a little boy who needs someone to love him. Here's a thought: Could I have been Florence Nightingale in a previous life? Here's another thought: Who am I going to be in my next life? Because I am still planning on a next life. Get that, God?

"Would you like me to explain the off-side rule?" asks Aunt Lou.

"8807494," says Ahim.

Definitely made the right decision getting out of his brain.

"Is that your number?" asks Aunt Lou. "Are you a convict?"

Ahim says nothing.

"The last one Martha brought home, Bill, he was a thief. He stole my silver tea strainer and my silver-backed hairbrushes."

"I'm not a thief," says Ahim.

"Does your religion forbid it?" asks Aunt Lou. "Oh, look at that," she shouts at the TV. "Get your glasses, ref!"

"I'm not a thief," repeats Ahim.

"Who are you then? Where do you come from? Why have you come here?"

"I'm . . .," says Ahim. "I'm"—and his head jerks—"*chosen*."

"Chosen?" repeats Aunt Lou. "Chosen for what? By whom? Exactly?"

"I'm sorry," Ahim says, shaking his head, just as he did before, as though he could dislodge the words. "I don't know what I say. Forgive me."

There's a pause.

"Well, you certainly chose to come here," says Aunt Lou dryly.

"I didn't choose here," says Ahim. "I come because Mrs. Laney asks me."

"So, what were you doing?" asks Aunt Lou. "Standing with a sign saying, Take me home, Mrs. Laney?"

"I was in a park," says Ahim. "They attacked me. Kicked me. Men."

Aunt Lou's brain fizz-cracks: *Liar. He's a liar.* "You don't look attacked," says Aunt Lou, "if I may say so."

"No," says Ahim.

I need a drink. Aunt Lou stands up. "Do you drink whiskey?" she asks.

"Men in liquor are no good to God," says Ahim.

"Good," says Aunt Lou and pours herself a large glass to which she does not add any water. She settles back down on the sofa and then stands up again to bring the half-full bottle to set on the table beside her. *Useful weapon, whiskey bottle,* she thinks.

The soccer commentator begins to get excited, the crowd yells, there's a great cross, a Manchester United striker poised in the box, and then—he's brought down. Penalty!

"What!" cries Aunt Lou. "Did you see that? He dived. Call that fair? Outrageous!"

She pours herself another whiskey. *I could do with a whiskey myself. Or at least something a bit wetter than Aunt Lou's brain. I don't think I can spend the night here. It would be too dangerous. I could dry out.*

The Man U player places the ball for the penalty. The whistle goes; he runs, strikes; the goalkeeper goes the wrong way; he scores!

"Right," says Aunt Lou. "We'll see about that." She begins to fast-forward the tape. She gets to halftime; no change in the score. Grimly she fast-forwards through the advertisements, and then on to the second half. In the eighty-seventh minute, Arsenal scores. Aunt Lou watches the goal and then replays it three times. It's a nifty little header from the Arsenal front man.

"That's what I call a goal," she says with satisfaction and drains her whiskey. She leans forward. "You see," she says to Ahim, "in life there's always a good team and a better team. A good god and a better god." *Ax-murderer,* she thinks.

Ahim says nothing.

Aunt Lou checks the end of the game to make sure there

are no more goals, which there aren't, and then she switches off the TV.

"Good-night," she says.

Quickly I exit her brain. She uses the bathroom, checks on Mary, and retreats to her room. I hear the noise of a lock turning.

Ahim gets up off the sofa and goes to the window, pulls the curtain aside. It is very dark out now, though the street-lights and the lit windows opposite throw yellow light into the air. Ahim looks up, high into the night sky, and I know, despite everything, that his brain is where I need to be.

I speed to his face and arrive in the fissure just in time to hear that same voice, sweet and clear, only this time the woman says: *God has a purpose for you, my son.* And it's such a sweet voice but, all of a sudden, the words seem chilling.

7

Mrs. Laney has laid out a clean towel, a washcloth, and a small honeysuckle guest soap still in its box. Ahim takes these items to the bathroom, locks the door, and begins to undress. Yes, you heard; he begins to undress. I'm in the head of some guy who's just about to strip naked. It makes me feel a little hot. And also invasive. I want to close my eyes, but of course I haven't got eyes and, do you know what? I can't shut my droplets off; just as I can't stop hearing, I can't stop seeing, the whole fist of me sees.

His shirt is off. His trousers are off. He's on to his socks. I slide out of the fissure and along his airways and out into the world. I shall hide behind Mrs. Laney's bright aquamarine shower curtain. Anything I see will be through a blur of blue. That's when Ahim comes to a stop, underpants still on. He doesn't wear boxers but those slimline pants French boys wear. I'm not telling you how I know that about French boys. Anyhow, the thing that's a surprise is Ahim's body.

I take up a position in front of the shower curtain. When I was at the train station, I can't say I gave much thought to Ahim's body; my mind was more on the debris and the dying. And, of course, tonight he's been well covered up with the baggy, ill-fitting clothes I think I mentioned before, the ones that look like he might have got them from the

Salvation Army. Anyway—his body. It's good, it's nice. He has beautiful, taut skin, and although he's slight, he looks lithe and strong. He's not at all muscly, but you can see the power in his upper arms and chest. Of course, he's not very tall but—hey, didn't I just get smaller recently?

I also take a proper look at his face. He has well-spaced features, a good nose, and a strong chin. His mouth has a smiling upturned curve. His eyes are brown and his jet-black hair has a little kick to it. You know—he's almost handsome.

"Not bad!" I say. Which, praise your god-of-choice, he doesn't hear.

He begins to wash. He runs a basinful of warm water and uses the soap and the washcloth on his hands and his upper body. He rinses himself meticulously, dries his arms and chest with the towel, and then he begins again, washing and drying his face. When he is quite clean, he stands with his feet apart and spreads the fingers of his left hand over the place where his heart is.

"J'lal, Holy, Only God, I submit to you." He removes the yellow-gold ring and brings it to his lips, kisses it, and then drops to his knees.

"Ingali, Holy Angel, touch of God's Hand, I revere you." He removes the white-gold ring and kisses that, too.

"A . . . Ah . . ." There's a pause, and for a moment I think he's just going to sneeze. And then he says, "Ahim," and I realize he's been struggling with his own name.

"Ahim," he begins again, using his name uncertainly. "Know this . . . Ahim . . . your God sees all your deeds, done and undone." He takes off the final ring but instead of kissing it, he just holds it in front of his eyes.

Then, bowing his head low, he says: "*Bi'marak istali, antab batak!*" He replaces all three rings on the middle finger of his left hand and stands up.

And of course I know it's just a ritual, and I guess all

religions have their rituals, like we make the sign of the cross in front of the altar. But here, in the bathroom, it looks a little tribal. Mind you, if Ahim came into a Christian church and watched the priests waltz about in long robes with gold tassels on or waft incense about or ring bells, it might look rather tribal to him. And what do I mean by "tribal" anyway, that it's just something that primitive people indulge in? How disrespectful is that? Do you think there's such a thing as a para-spirit library, where you can go and improve your knowledge, or at least your respect? No, maybe not. Perhaps we're back with tribes meaning groups again, the Nike Sneaker People; we do it this way because that's what our tribe does. I don't know. I wish I could have lived a bit longer and found a few more things out. My ignorance is near total. I suppose all I'm observing is faith, this T'lanni's faith in his god. But that's another weird thing: If he believed in Leo the zodiac lion or Aquarius the water-bearer, you'd call it superstition, wouldn't you? So what makes belief in astrology superstition and belief in God, faith?

Ahim re-dresses, for modesty I suppose, and returns to the living room. He closes the curtains and unfolds his bedding; there's a sheet, a pillow, and a comforter in an eccentric brown swirly pattern that makes it look like some refugee from the Sixties. Ahim tucks the sheet in around the cushions of the larger red sofa and plumps up the pillow. He lays the comforter down with care and precision. Then he drops to the floor.

For a moment I think he's going to do some push-ups, but he lies quite still with his face flat to the carpet and his arms outstretched.

"*Hakamdaba!*" he declares.

Do you think it's just because I can't understand him, it seems so weird? Is it partly a matter of language? I fling myself to the floor beside him.

"Abracadabra!" I shout.

Nothing happens. I'm still a ball of mist.

No, correction, something does happen: I feel like I've just blasphemed. Sorry, Ahim. Sorry, God of Ahim.

Ahim stands up and begins to take off his trousers. Time to retreat, behind the sofa or into the brain? Brain, I think. Would you sleep naked with Aunt Lou in the house? No. Good thinking, Ahim. He climbs into bed with his underpants firmly on.

It's good to be back in the fissure. I allow myself to expand a little, drink in a little moisture. Ahim's brain is quiet, no zapping numbers, no chosen this and chosen that. Maybe the prayer rituals have calmed him down. I feel I ought to try and get to sleep right away, in case the numbers start again. It's the same sense of urgency I had when I went camping with my friend Bella. I had to get to sleep before she did because she snored. So, of course, I couldn't get to sleep at all, which is about the same as now.

Ahim tosses and turns. I toss and turn; well, revolve slightly in the fissure. Of course it's dark, and there isn't much to see as Ahim has his eyelids closed, but I am still "seeing," which of course makes me feel awake. Very awake actually. Maybe that doze in Bonnie was all I needed. It could be that para-spirits don't need much sleep. Perhaps, in fact, dozing is as good as it gets for para-spirits. That would be depressing. There's something beautiful about sleep, I've always thought, that wonderful moment when you lie down and let slumber take you softly away, knowing tomorrow will be a bright new day.

Ahim stops tossing, his breathing becomes slower, easier, he snuggles beneath the comforter, he is asleep.

And I am awake.

Awake.

Awake.

Awake.

When I was alive and this awake, I used to turn on my light and read. The equivalent in Ahim's brain is probably a little exploring. So off I go, edging out of the fissure and sliding over the surface of his lobes. Nothing to see in his visual cortex, of course, and a complete blank in his memory region. I wish I had a little spade and then I could dig down and see what lies beneath his forgetting. No, no, I don't mean that, of course. I know my place. No interfering. But he must have forgotten, mustn't he? Maybe the bomb, or maybe the kicking, have resulted in amnesia. But if he's lost his memory, how come he remembers his prayers? And also how to be polite? Yes, Aunt Lou. No, Aunt Lou. Three bags full, Aunt Lou. But maybe that's how it works. I remember my great-aunt Dorothy and how she had precise memories of things that had happened in her childhood, but no idea what she'd had for breakfast.

I'm just moseying around Ahim's brain, thinking my innocent thoughts, when someone turns the radio on. At first I think Mrs. Laney must have returned because there it is, clear and well-tuned, the first two lines of Eric Clapton's "Tears in Heaven." I know the song well because, in the far-off days when I used to have a piano and a piano teacher, I used to play it. Only the easy version, of course, but Miss Turpin told me about the song, how Clapton wrote it after his four-year-old son Conor fell to his death from his apartment building. It's a beautiful, haunting tune, and of course it's not on the radio at all. It's here, floating across the surface of Ahim's brain. And why is that so hard for me to imagine? Because I think if there's music in Ahim's brain, it will be foreign music, something I haven't heard, don't understand? When was the song written? 1992, I think. How old would Ahim have been? Sixteen, maybe seventeen? Ahim, youngster, citizen of the world, my world. Not such a stranger after all. I wonder what other songs his sleeping mind will play. Perhaps I have a good night ahead of me after all; Ahim and me, we can sing, dance, boogie, rock.

I'm just getting in the mood, beginning a little haunting sway, when I'm assaulted by a wash—no, a tidal wave—of anxiety. The emotion is quite distinct and at first I think it comes from the song, but it doesn't, it's much more personal than that. And nor is *anxiety* quite the right word, either; the feeling is too sharp, it's more like panic. Then I realize that actually the music has stopped and in its place a color has come, two colors in fact: the brilliant blue of a cloudless summer sky and the hot yellow of blazing sand or sun. Quite the wrong colors for such dazzling panic. The emotion and the colors don't hurt in the physical sense that the fizz-cracks hurt, but they do hurt, right deep inside me. But I don't attempt to move, partly because I don't think I would have protection from these feelings even if I was to return to the fissure.

So I just wait, and after a while, some pictures come. They come like an ink stain comes, or like a bruise taking shape on your leg when you've been kicked, spreading slowly and in strange unpredictable shapes. The blue color concentrates and I think it is sky but it is also turrets, it's spires; and the yellow, which is sand and sun, is also the gold on the palaces that are swimming in Ahim's mind. For that's what's arising from this mirage of colors—more colors coming now, a bleached white, a silver, a mud red—and it's a town, a city even, something drawn from the imagination of a child, or dreamed up by a genie for Aladdin, an Eastern city rising like a hill, baked by the sun, close enough for you to see the faces in the streets and yet also somehow far away, out of reach, magical. I think it quite beautiful, but in Ahim's mind there is only the drumming: anxiety, fear.

Then, lying across the sand in front of the city, I see a huge black snake. The snake is twisting, moving oh-so-slowly forward. And I think maybe it's this that so frightens Ahim, but then the snake unwinds, or maybe I just see it better, and it's cars, only a line of cars waiting to get in at the gate. For there is a gate. I don't know how I missed the gate and the glinting silver barrier beside it: wire, barbed wire, rolls and rolls of it, higher than a man. The sun reflects so prettily on it.

I've only just grasped these new images when there's a jolt, a shift; the snake of cars whips like a tail and then shrinks, concentrates until there is just one car, an old car, dusty, stopped at the barrier. We're viewing the scene from behind. There are three people in the car, the backs of their bodies come into gradual focus: an old woman, veiled and garmented entirely in black; a younger woman in Western clothes; and, behind them, in the backseat, a small dark-haired child, a girl.

From a squat gray hut beyond the barbed wire, a soldier appears. There's another jolt, not in the pictures this time, but in Ahim's emotions. I feel it like a stab. The soldier is in desert fatigues with his metal helmet pulled down over his eyes. There's a pistol at his waist and a small machine gun strapped across his chest. His right hand rests on its butt.

He comes to the car. "Passes," he says.

The young woman hands three small squares of paper through the driver's window.

The soldier examines the passes and then stares at each occupant of the car in turn, even the child. "Your business in Sacrini?"

"I'm taking my mother to the hospital," says the young woman. "It's her legs, she has bad legs."

The soldier looks at the old woman and then, quite deliberately, drops one of the passes into the sand at his feet. "Oops," he says.

I see, because Ahim sees, a slight tension in the young woman's neck. But she says nothing, just begins to open the car door, to get out, to retrieve the pass.

"No," says the soldier. "It's not your pass." He nods at the old woman. "It's hers."

"She can barely walk," exclaims the young woman, then she clasps her hand to her mouth, drops her eyes to the ground.

"Get back in the car," the soldier orders.

The young woman obeys, she sits, she shuts the door.

For a moment, no one moves, not even the child. I feel tight inside, like I had breath and was holding it.

"What the hell are you waiting for, old woman?" The soldier thrusts the barrel of the machine gun through the window of the car. "You want to make me angry?"

The old woman, who looks like a black ghost, turns stiffly to open the car door on her side. Slowly she shuffles her body around, so that she can put both feet to the ground. As she pulls herself out of the door, I hear a small sigh of pain. Ahim's head needles.

"You think we have all day? Get a move on." The soldier bangs his fist on the roof of the car. The child in the back shrinks down a little and begins a snuffly sob.

"And you can shut up."

"Shush, Esta," says the mother, but she doesn't turn around.

The old woman walks with difficulty around the front of the car, her left leg drags slightly, and she has to pause twice to regain her balance. When she finally reaches the soldier, he nudges the pass with his foot. "Go on then." The old woman bends down. I hear her knees crack. She wobbles, but steadies herself; reaches for the pass. As her hands touch the paper, the soldier's foot comes down, crushing her fingers. The old woman gives a stifled yelp, like a puppy in pain whose mouth is being held closed.

"Oh," says the soldier, "sorry." And he laughs.

"Gan-gan!" cries the child.

"Shush," says the mother.

Then things begin to slip and slide. The soldier disappears, the car and its occupants move forward through the barrier into a kind of no-man's-land between the barbed wire barrier and a wall. The wall is huge and black but not solid; it has a hazy, miasmic quality, like in a dream. And that's when I realize what this is: it's Ahim's dream. He dreams the car a little further, and I feel he wants to dream it further still, to send the car along the road into the city unhindered. But there's a sound in his head like muffled blood, the beat of your heart when panic drums in your ears. And then it comes, a sudden appalling burst of semi-automatic gunfire. It rips through the desert air.

In the front seat of the car, the younger woman jerks at the wheel, her head pitched left and right. The car swerves violently, and the child in the back is hurled up to the roof. I see her little body flail, and then there's another burst of fire. The old woman doesn't move at all.

Then the dream skews. The car skids to a stop, and I hear a car door slam, only it's not slamming shut, but somehow slamming open, and the child is flung out onto the no-man's-land sand. She falls and twists and lies there, and for the first time I see her face. It's Aelfin's face. And I cry out. I can't help myself; it's my sister lying dead in the desert. And then there's another screech, but much smaller this time, like the sound of a tape jamming in a cassette machine. Aelfin disappears, there's no one on the ground at all. I'm back behind the car which is moving again, skidding again, and for a second time the door slams open. A tiny body spins and falls again, lies in the dirt. This time it's Mary.

In his sleep Ahim writhes and moans, his brain tearing at itself and at the images. And then the car door begins to swing maniacally, out, in, out, in, and the bodies come twisting and falling, only as soon as they land in the sand they spin back into the car again, Aelfin, Mary, Aelfin, Mary—and then finally a different body comes, and when this child lands and turns toward me, she has no face at all.

"Aaargh!"

The scream is acute and childish. It rips through Ahim's brain. He pulls himself upright, wide awake and trembling.

"Aaargh!" the scream comes again. And it is not the scream of the dream, it is a real scream, coming from the apartment.

Ahim leaps up, throwing aside the comforter, and in an instant he is out in the hall.

Where is she? his brain synapses. *Where is she?*

Quickly I move back into the fissure.

"Esta!" he cries, and he bursts into Mary's room.

Mary is sitting up in bed wide-eyed with fright. Her body is stiff and shaking.

"What is it?" cries Ahim.

"I dreamed," shouts Mary. "I dreamed . . . I dreamed the Daddy dream!"

"Esta," Ahim says. "Oh, Esta."

He sits down on the side of the bed.

"No," says Mary. "No, go away. I want my mommy. Mommy!" she shrieks and bursts into tears.

Aunt Lou arrives at the door with Bister.

"Ax-murderer!" she shouts, candlewick dressing gown on, eyes ablaze. "What do you think you're doing?"

"She has dreams," says Ahim calmly. "Bad dreams. So, of course, I am here." He is looking at Mary but seeing the girl with no face. He's not in this room at all, I think, not part of whatever it is that troubles Mary, he's still in some nightmare of his own.

"Leave her alone!" says Aunt Lou. "Don't touch her!"

Bister yaps, he growls. Aunt Lou holds on to his collar.

"I'm not touching her," says Ahim.

But he is. He's sitting on the bed and, even though Mary is pulling away, he is very desperately, very gently, trying to stroke her hand.

8

In the living room, Ahim sits on the sofa and puts his head in his hands. Across the corridor Mary's sobbing eventually subsides. In the silence that follows, I hear Aunt Lou walking up and down and then the sound of something being stacked against the living room door. Maybe she's barricading Ahim in, maybe she's just put something there that will fall and wake her if he tries to leave the room.

Ahim gets up and paces. *Esta*, his brain says, Esta. There's a stirring in his memory lobes and then a picture comes. It's a young girl with bronzed limbs wearing a loose, bleached-out yellow dress. She has her back to Ahim. Ahim shakes his head; but this time I have the feeling that far from wanting to dislodge this memory, Ahim seeks to spin the girl around, to see her more clearly, but she remains turned away.

Esta, his brain synapses again. Inside his skull there is a tension, I feel a kind of pull, as if the side of the brain where I am is desperately trying to draw something from the memory-lobe side. For a moment the girl hovers; she's almost dancing, curtsying in the sand, and then she does turn. Her face is a hole. Ahim shakes his head fiercely once again, balls his hands into fists, and strikes his forehead.

Pray, God, he thinks, *let me remember*.

His brain goes black, as if someone switched him off at the

plug, and then, almost immediately, he fizzes back into life again but the color remains: black. I think at first the color is all around, like a night sky, but then I realize it is actually the color of a gigantic object that is, very swiftly, contracting. As the object gets smaller and smaller it begins to take on a brassy metallic sheen. When the thing is no bigger than a thumb, I realize what it is: it's a bullet.

"No, not this!" cries Ahim, and I think it will be the bullet fired at the girl who dances in the sand, but no, the child in these pictures is a boy. He can only be about four or five, and he's standing at the edge of an olive grove with a slingshot in his hands. The handle of the slingshot is made of metal. Behind the boy are acres of beautiful gray-green trees. Men and women are beating the trees with sticks and collecting the hard green olives as they fall. In front of the boy are the barbed wire and the no-man's-land sand and a wall. This time the wall is solid and dark and topped with gun turrets. The boy puts something small and wet and white into the leather part of the slingshot, and inexpertly draws back the heavy elastic, prepares to fire. White stuff (paint?) oozes onto his thumb and forefinger.

Pictures flurry then, coming ferociously fast, like my mother's memories came, playing on more than one screen at once, and with them the sound of gunfire. On the largest screen there is the bullet, advancing toward the boy. The moment its tip touches the boy's cotton shirt, a woman comes into the picture: she drops her stick and her basket of olives and flings herself across the boy, as though she would kiss him. But the bullet keeps on coming, slowly but with deadly accuracy. The boy falls, and as he does so he puts his hand up to his breast as if to feel the blood. But there is no blood, there is no wound. The bullet disintegrates; I watch it dissolve against the boy's chest. And he watches it, too.

On a nearby screen a larger boy with a wooden sling-shot comes running, panting, yelling: "Akim! Akim! Come on, come away!" and he grabs the little boy's hand, dragging him deep into the olive grove. On the final screen there is a picture of the little boy with his tiny black-haired head buried in a woman's skirts. "They shot at him," the elder boy says. "They shot at him, Mama, and he survived."

The woman pulls the boy from her body: "Look at me, Akim," she says. The boy's wide eyes are on her. "You are alive. God is good. You are chosen, Akim. God has a purpose for you, my son. *Antab batak!*" Her voice is sweet and clear.

In Martha Laney's living room, Ahim slumps down on the sofa, pushes his feet under the comforter, and curls up into a fetal ball. In his head is the crump of an explosion, not a fizz-crack or a synapse, but the sound I heard at the train station, just before all the glass shattered. Ahim draws himself even tighter in, arms crossed over his breast, hugging his shoulders. The explosion repeats, only louder.

Let me not remember, Ahim thinks. *Pray God that I don't remember.*

He grits his teeth and does not sleep. I don't sleep, either. The explosions continue for an hour, maybe two hours; but gradually the lulls between each bang get longer. When it seems that the blasts may finally have stopped altogether, I feel Ahim's body lengthen; he is exhausted. I'm not exhausted, not physically anyway, though I feel worn out with the roller coaster of Ahim's dreams, and also with my own thudding memories of that day at the station.

I fall into a kind of fitful doze. I remember Blacoe's use of the word *nap*. He wanted to nap when Dad was going to drive home, presumably because Dad's thoughts would be on the journey and so his brain would be comparatively peaceful. Napping, not sleeping. I'm beginning to believe that's something I'm going to have to get used to. Do you think you can get used to anything if you must? Do you think if I said there would be no green grass in the world tomorrow, or no one would be able to sit down ever again, only stand or lie, do you think we'd all survive, make do? So many things it seems I've taken for granted.

There's a light snuffle from Ahim's nose. He is finally asleep, and I envy him. But perhaps that's only cowardice. Perhaps, just for a while, I want to do some forgetting of my own. Forget I'm dead; forget I allowed myself to get separated from Mom and Dad and Bonnie; forget that Aelfin's gone who knows where; just forget, wake up to a brand new day. But I guess there isn't a brand new day for me right now, only the morning after the night before. And it's almost morning now.

Mary is first up. I hear her pad into the living room, Bister beside her. She must have dismantled Aunt Lou's barricade because there is no noise of falling and therefore no response from along the corridor. There is not much response from Ahim, either, even when she switches on the television. He just mumbles and turns over. I drift out of Ahim's head, partly for the change of scene, and partly because I can't see anything when Ahim has his eyelids closed. Mary, who's clearly forgotten Ahim's presence, jumps when she sees him stir; but other than pulling Bister closer to her, she does nothing, neither moving from the sofa nor turning the program's volume down.

I hover around the back of the sofa and watch cartoons with Mary. I've never quite grown out of cartoons. These are good, some of them are laugh-out-loud funny, although Mary doesn't laugh. I wish I could laugh out loud. I wish I could laugh, period. I make a resolution: If I ever get back to being a human being, I'm going to laugh a whole lot more. I'm going to try and laugh about every twenty minutes. Being at school should pretty much see to that.

Hey—school. Be positive, Cassina. At least you're not at school now. Life is good. Para-life anyway.

Ahim sleeps on for a scant six minutes and then wakes quite suddenly. He sits up, sees Mary, clutches his trousers to him, and makes for the bathroom. I abandon the cartoons and go with him, entering his head again, being grateful for the moisture. I observe Ahim's morning ablutions and the ritual with the rings. Do you think if you said the same prayers twice a day, they would become more meaningful or less meaningful? Would they be the most uplifting part of your daily life or, after a while, would you just be going through the motions, thinking not about God but about breakfast? I think I'd be thinking about breakfast, but Ahim isn't. Mind you, he's not thinking about the prayers, either. His brain is like a computer in safety mode: the picture pale and not quite right.

He puts on his shabby clothes and returns to the living room. Mrs. Laney is up now, and so is Aunt Lou.

"Good morning, Ahim," says Mrs. Laney brightly. "Did you sleep well?" She has cleared away his bedding and set the alcove table for breakfast.

"Thank you," says Ahim. "Yes."

Aunt Lou, in a dark purple suit and white blouse flecked with face powder, eyes him suspiciously.

"My aunt tells me how concerned you were for Mary," says Mrs. Laney, "when she had her bad dream. It was kind of you, Ahim." She lowers her voice. "She does have bad dreams, my Mary."

"Yes," says Ahim. "I, too, have dreams. Bad dreams." He looks at Mary. "What do you dream, child?"

"Nothing," says Mary.

"A recurrent dream," answers Mrs. Laney quickly, giving him an adult look to stop him inquiring further. "What about you?"

"I dream," says Ahim. "I see . . . I think I see things no man should have to see."

"Well, we won't talk about that then, will we," says Aunt Lou.

The morning progresses at a weekend pace; the television is turned off, and breakfast is eaten. Mrs. Laney remains bright; Aunt Lou, sullenly aggressive; and Mary, detached. When the table is cleared, Mrs. Laney says, "Well. Ahim, I think we should have a discussion about your future, don't you?"

And I think that on a similar sort of Saturday morning in my house, my mother might have said, "What shall we do today, girls?" And Aelfi and I might have mentioned friends to play with or places to go or gymnastics practice. It strikes me then that I don't see any evidence here of a child's life for Mary. No activities, no places to go, no friends. Mind you, would you want to invite friends back to this apartment? "Olivia, meet my mad aunt Lou, you'll really like her. She's a scream." No wonder Mary has bad dreams.

"I'll go and get the newspapers then," says Aunt Lou.

"We need to find your family," Mrs. Laney says to Ahim, getting out a large sheet of lined writing paper and a ballpoint pen. She sits down at the table.

"I'll go with Aunt Lou," says Mary. Biggest adventure of her week, no doubt. I wonder if the two of them ever play with her, her mother, Aunt Lou? Somehow I can't quite imagine it; Mrs. Laney, too busy saving the world, and Aunt Lou, too busy saving the whiskey. There aren't even any toys in this room and, yes, I know it's the sitting room, but my cousin Toby, who's also about seven, manages to spread his toys over the whole house. Oh, hang on, there's a wooden solitaire board up on the shelf, behind the table, an old-fashioned one with marbles on it. Maybe Aunt Lou plays that with Mary. No, solitaire's a game for one, isn't it? Solitaire. Solitaire Mary. I'd like to play with her, I think suddenly; I'd like to hear her laugh.

Bister begins to bark then; at least Mary's got him. I've found there's a lot you can talk to a dog about. Bister obviously considers himself part of the newspaper team, too. The incongruous threesome leaves, and Ahim sits down at the table.

"Now," says Mrs. Laney, sucking the pen end, "can you tell me your surname, Ahim?"

But of course he can't, although his brain tenses, as if he's trying once again to draw something from his memory. Yet there are no synapses, no pictures of any clarity.

"No," he says. "Sorry."

"Do you remember if you've always lived here, in this country, or if maybe you came here as a child?"

The barbed wire comes, the city, the wall. "No," he says quickly.

"What about how old you are, when you were born? We might be able to trace a birth certificate."

He tries to locate these details. His brain pulls and claws at itself.

"No," he says.

"Never mind," says Mrs. Laney. "Let's concentrate on your family. You must remember something about them: brothers, sisters . . ."

"Esta," says Ahim.

"Esta," repeats Mrs. Laney. "Wonderful. Is she your sister?"

The faceless child in the loose yellow dress dances in the no-man's-land sand.

"No."

"Your mother?"

"No. I think . . . I think Esta is my child." When he says

"my child," a hollowness comes into his brain like the whole world disappeared down a hole.

"So you must be married?" Mrs. Laney says.

There's a picture of the back of the young woman's head at the checkpoint. Then there's a fizz-crack which says hospital and a picture of a peacefully beautiful woman lying whiter than the sheets she is surrounded by.

"We'll try missing persons," Mrs. Laney continues. "If you have a child, you must have a wife and she could well have reported you missing. We'll ring the police."

"No," says Ahim suddenly.

"Why not?"

"08894407." The numbers blot out the dancing girl and the white woman. They are hot and insistent; they flash across Ahim's brain.

"What is that number, Ahim? It's the one you said yesterday, isn't it? When we were in the park. Are you in the army? Is it an army number?"

"08894407814."

As he speaks Mrs. Laney writes the number down. "Could be a phone number. Is it a phone number, Ahim?" She gets up and lifts an old-fashioned cream-colored phone from the sideboard, uncurls the twisted socket wire, and brings it to the table. "Why don't you try dialing it?"

Ahim cradles the receiver in his left hand for a moment and stares at the big square numbers on the main body of the phone as if he has no idea what they are. But he dials nonetheless, and when he finally puts the receiver to his ear, he is breathing hard.

The number-unavailable tone is so harsh even I hear it.

"No," says Ahim, relieved. But in his brain the numbers are still coming, they are reforming, reshaping, arranging themselves into a different order.

"Well, then!" Aunt Lou bursts triumphantly into the

apartment. "No need to wonder any more who Ahim is!" She strides across the living room and throws a newspaper down onto the table.

Mary, following in Aunt Lou's wake, looks flushed and anxious. Bister barks excitedly.

"What's this, Aunt Lou?" Mrs. Laney asks exasperated. The newspaper has landed on her notepad.

"Look. Just look!" shouts Aunt Lou, and she jabs her finger on the main front-page article. Under the headline "Bomb Suspects" are two black-and-white photographs. The left-hand photo is of a man in his early thirties who stares at the camera with a mixture of hostility and triumph. He's tall, and his face is hard and handsome.

"'Habril Fazheen,'" reads Mrs. Laney. "'Suspected mastermind behind station bomb.'"

"Not that one," shouts Aunt Lou. "The other one!"

The second photograph is of a smaller, slighter man, with a smiling upturn to his mouth and a slight kick to his hair.

"'Akim Watabi,'" reads Mrs. Laney, "'the suspected suicide bomber.'"

Aunt Lou pulls the paper down in front of Ahim.

"That's you, isn't it?" she asks.

"Akim," repeats Ahim slowly. "Akim Watabi." And then his brain fires: *Know this, Akim Watabi, your God sees all your deeds, done and undone.*

"Aunt Lou," says Mrs. Laney sternly, "don't you see anything faintly ridiculous in accusing Ahim of being a suicide bomber?"

"No," says Aunt Lou.

In Ahim's brain there's the crump, crump of an explosion and some shattering glass.

"It's definitely him," says Aunt Lou.

"It looks like him, a bit, doesn't it, Ahim?" says Mary. "It does look a bit like you."

"Yes," says Ahim.

"Only if it was really him," says Mrs. Laney, "then he wouldn't be here, would he? He'd be dead. That's the nature of suicide-bombing. You get killed."

"Some of them survive," says Aunt Lou grumpily.

"Not if the bomb goes off, Aunt Lou."

"Some of them are 'chosen,'" says Aunt Lou.

"Ahim, please excuse my aunt."

"44088," says Ahim. "078149." He snatches the pen from Mrs. Laney, who gasps a little oh of surprise, and begins scribbling frantically on the newspaper beside the picture of Habril Fazheen.

"You see," says Aunt Lou, "he even has his phone number."

"814944088," writes Ahim. "14944088078."

"If it's a mobile number," says Mary helpfully, "it will begin with the 078 bit. At least that's how Uncle Ted's does."

"07814944088," writes down Ahim. He looks at the number and then at the photograph. His brain fizz-cracks. "It is. That's it." He drops the pen. His hands are trembling.

Grimly Aunt Lou hands the phone to him. "Go on," she says. "Dial it."

Ahim looks at Aunt Lou, he looks at Mrs. Laney, he looks at Mary.

"Go on," says Mrs. Laney. "Why not?"

Ahim takes the phone. I wouldn't like to be in his heart chamber; I can hear the blood thumping even here in his brain. This time he touches the keypad swiftly and with a practiced precision, as if it's a number he's dialed many times. That seems to calm him. He puts the phone to his ear.

The tone rings. If I had breath, I'd be holding it.

I hear a click on the line; the phone has been picked up, but no one speaks.

"Hello," says Ahim.

"Who's this?" questions a harsh voice on the other end.

"It's me," says Ahim quietly.

"Akim?" queries the voice. "Akim!"

"Yes," whispers Ahim. "I think so."

"*Antab batak!*" shouts the voice. "Holy, Holy Lord! It's Akim," he shouts to someone at his end of the call. "Akim's alive!"

Ahim says nothing.

"Where are you?" demands the voice.

The man who was Ahim gives the address.

9

I can't say I didn't have my suspicions. I mean he's a T'lanni; he was in the right place (the train station) at the right time (when the bomb went off); plus—what's his first memory when the amnesia begins to clear? The crump of explosions, that's what. So I wasn't exactly short on clues. So how come I was resisting the information, refusing to believe that my friend Ahim (and I want to keep calling him Ahim for a moment) could actually be my murderer?

Of course, there is Mrs. Laney's point: if Ahim was the suicide bomber, then he'd be dead, right? However, if you accept (and as a para-spirit I have to) that I ended up half alive after the bombing, it's not really such a stretch to think of him ending up wholly alive. And while this might not rate as a scientific explanation, I think we've gone beyond science here. Or as my Hamlet-obsessed English teacher would constantly tell her attentive class, "There are more things in heaven and earth, Horatio, than are dreamed of in your philosophy."

Nevertheless, I still allowed myself to fool myself. Why? Because Ahim doesn't look like the bad guy? Would it have been easier if he'd burst into my life in a green glittery cloak shouting, "Ha, ha, ha, I'll get you, see if I don't!"? Or if he'd sported a black Hitleresque mustache and worn a sandwich board with the slogan "Hi, I'm evil" painted on it? Surely I'm smart enough not to always judge a book by its cover. But Ahim? Quiet-spoken, polite Ahim? The gentle, handsome guy with the nice body, the one who likes Eric Clapton songs and who happened to spend his childhood scrabbling around olive groves with a slingshot? The young man who probably had a dancing desert daughter who came to a not-so-pleasant end? It doesn't quite add up. I mean—I like the guy. There is another possibility, of course: Ahim isn't actually evil. But how can someone who walks into a train station, intent on blowing up anyone who happens to be there, not be evil?

I decide to take a trip to Ahim's heart. Directly after the attack in the park, his heart chamber was quiet but otherwise normal—I mean his heart didn't look substantially different from my dad's. I need to know if that's still the case, or if I can now tell that this is the heart of a murderer.

Ahim's breathing normally now, so it's more difficult to get into the lungs, but I'm determined and I'm soon riding my little blood sac to the left ventricle. The chamber is red and thumping. Ahim is no longer in a state of hibernation. (Is that how he survives these death situations, his body just temporarily closes down?) In fact his heart is beating loudly, almost joyously, I'd say. It's like being next to the drums of some tribe who have just annihilated the enemy. De-dum, de-dum, victory! De-dum, de-dum. Victory! Victory! De-dum, de-dum . . . It angers me. In fact, quite suddenly I feel furious. And maybe, of course, it's just my imagination, and it's not really a victory thump at all, maybe the beats are in fact no louder than the beats of my father's heart. But they sound louder. All of me reverberates with them, the heartbeats of my murderer. Because he did murder me. My droplets are pulsing. This man murdered me! I stretch myself out, long and thin and tight. Maybe I will be able to encircle his heart, maybe if I clench what's left of myself about him, I'll be able to squeeze the breath from his body. I will kill him as he killed me, as he killed Aelfin, as he killed all those others at the station. How many? I don't even know: twenty, eighty, a hundred? All of them human beings like me, who had a right to live, who weren't the ones who gunned down his family in no-man's-land, people who weren't involved . . . I concentrate my drops; it's not easy because I'm so strung out, and I fear the chain of me will break, that I'll snap apart around him and then what?

Who cares then what? What have I got to lose?

I concentrate myself, I am a noose around his heart, I tighten the band of me, pull against myself, but his heart still swells, his blood keeps pumping. De-dum, de-dum . . . I pull harder; it's difficult but I also feel a flush of excitement. Did Ahim tremble like this when he put his finger on the detonator of the bomb? Then I remember Mac when he was attacking Ahim; Mac with his heavy boots and flared nostrils and lathered-up look, and I think, what am I doing?

But it's too late.

Not for Ahim, whose heart is still pumping ferociously, but for me: I have broken, burst about him, little bits of myself flung wide. Way to go; maybe I'm really going to die this time.

As I scrabble and clutch for myself, I think, *You deserve this, Cassina. Where did your high-mindedness go exactly? If you're into revenge, you're no better than they are. No better than Mac. No better than Ahim. You deserve to die.* But then something strange happens: as well as the main body of me reaching for the droplets which have separated away from me, I feel those far broken-away droplets returning, almost as though each one had a will of its own, and that will was to be with and for me. In a very little time I am whole again. And, as I lie prone and pulsing in the dark blood-red chamber of Ahim's heart, I am glad. Grateful even.

I've been given another chance.

When I feel strong enough, I return up the aorta into my murderer's head. I have to go straight to the fissure because his brain is a maelstrom of images and emotions. For a moment I think maybe my pressure around his heart has had some effect after all, and then, on the memory screens, I see what he's thinking.

He observes himself standing on the station concourse, close to the ticket office which was the epicenter of the explosion. Beneath his clothes is the carefully sewn belt. He can feel nails, gunpowder, a battery, a light switch, some short cable, acetone, and eight pockets of explosives.

Words crisscross his mind like a chant. *The first drop of blood shed by a martyr is a kiss on the hand of God. And J'lal said: "Ingali, bring me the souls of the martyrs, for them I love, they shall be with me in Paradise forever."*

Ahim puts his hand over the light switch.

Paradise, he hears, *is very near—right in front of your eyes. It lies beneath the thumb. On the other side of the detonator.*

Ahim, in his memory, is not fired up at all. He is absolutely calm.

That's when I get out of his brain; I slide out into the open air. I can bear it no longer. I will not witness that bomb again, hear its noise, listen to the shattering of the glass, or watch again the twist of Aelfin's body.

I know it's fleeing, but I don't care. I tremble in the air of Mrs. Laney's living room. Mary is there, Aunt Lou is there, and Mrs. Laney herself.

Of course I will go into Mrs. Laney's brain. I imagine there will be some other para-spirit there, perhaps this is what's stopped me investigating before, because Mrs. Laney is a good, faithful, trusting person, why wouldn't you want to lodge in her brain?

"Clearly, it's an error," Mrs. Laney is saying to Ahim, her

finger pointing at the photo. "It's outrageous. Where do you think they got the picture from? You'll have to complain. It could make things very dangerous for you. They'll have to print a retraction."

Mrs. Laney's fissure is empty.

"Yes," says Ahim.

I am all alone inside Mrs. Laney, and grateful again.

"Did your friend say he was coming?" Mrs. Laney asks. "Will he pick you up?"

"Yes," says Ahim.

"I'm so glad you remembered the number. Is he a family member or a friend?"

"He's the suspect, the mastermind suspect," says Aunt Lou. "Habril Fazheen."

"Yes, thank you, Aunt Lou." Mrs. Laney's brain fizz-cracks: *She's getting worse. Aunt Lou's delusions are definitely getting worse. I think it really is dementia this time. Is any one of you sick? He should call the elders of the church to pray over him and anoint him with oil in the name of the Lord. James, Chapter Five, Verse Fourteen. Dear Lord, please don't let it be dementia for Aunt Lou. She's a very nice person really. Very kind-natured. Perhaps I should also make an appointment with the doctor?* "Ahim?"

"A friend," says Ahim.

"Will you be able to stay with him, will it be all right?"

"Yes," says Ahim, "thank you."

There is a ring at the door phone. Bister barks uncontrollably.

"Be quiet, be quiet, Bister," shouts Mrs. Laney. "Sorry," she adds, "we don't get so many visitors."

Mrs. Laney buzzes the door phone, waits for the elevator, and opens the door. When she returns it's with Habril Fazheen.

"Told you so," says Aunt Lou.

Bister growls.

"Of course," says Mrs. Laney, "if there's one wrong photo there could be two. We were talking about the photos," she adds, addressing Habril, "the newspapers. Ridiculous." She valiantly pushes the paper toward him, but her hands are trembling. In her brain is a little green flash. *Doubt*, it says. *Oh my Lord*, it says, adding quickly, *do not be anxious about anything, but in everything, by prayer and petition, with thanksgiving, present your requests to God. Philippians, Chapter Four, Verse Six.* Then there's a pause: *God?*

Habril is not paying any attention to the newspaper, he is not paying any attention to Mrs. Laney or Aunt Lou. He is staring only at Ahim. He crosses the room, stands directly in front of Ahim, and clasps him by both shoulders. I see his hands pressing Ahim's flesh, hard enough, I think, to feel if there is bone beneath. Then he moves his hand and cups Ahim's face, his fingers on Ahim's cheek.

"It's a miracle," he says. "Holy Lord, a miracle. *Antab batak.*" There are tears in his eyes.

Ahim moves then, he holds up his left hand, and swiftly Habril meets it with his own left hand. I hear the clash of their rings. "*Salanika,*" they say together. "*Salanika,* my brother."

"Are you brothers?" says Mary, who has been watching with curious eyes.

"Would you like tea?" asks Mrs. Laney with some desperation.

"Why do you bomb us?" asks Aunt Lou.

Habril turns around. "I bomb no one." He's wearing a short black leather jacket which he puts his hand inside. I may have watched too many movies in my short life, but I can't help wondering if he has a gun tucked in there.

"Do you do it because your people are poor?" asks Aunt Lou.

"My people are not poor," ripostes Habril. "Your people

are poor. You have televisions in your eyes and degenerate music in your ears and rich food in your bellies, but in your souls you have nothing. You are empty."

"I agree," says Mrs. Laney quickly. "Far too many of us in the West judge ourselves by how big our houses are, not how big our hearts are."

Habril stares at her, as if this is the first time he's noticed her in the room.

"So why do you do it?" asks Mary. "The suicide bombs?"

"Sacred explosions," says Habril.

"Sacred explosions!" says Aunt Lou. "You kill people. You kill yourselves. Kill your young men and women."

"They are youth at the peak of their blooming," says Habril, "who, at a certain moment, decide to turn their bodies into body parts, into flowers."

"You're crazy," says Aunt Lou. "You're mad. I'm going to call the police."

Habril takes his hand out of his jacket. It's empty—but it's a strong hand. He rips the cream phone from the socket in the wall.

Mary gives a little gasp, and Mrs. Laney's brain skids with fear. At once she moves to protect her daughter, putting herself between Mary and Habril.

Habril looks at the women and laughs. Then he pulls the wire from the back of the phone.

"There's a child here," says Ahim. "Beware the child, Habril."

"There are children in our country, Akim. When have children ever mattered?"

And in Ahim's clouded eyes, I think I see the girl again, the one that dances in the sand.

"These are good people, Habril. These people helped me. Brought me to their home. Looked after me. Is this how I am to repay their hospitality?"

Habril puts down the phone, smooths the wire, and pulls two twenty-pound notes from inside his jacket. "Forgive me," he says stiffly, offering Mrs. Laney the money. "I am forgetting myself. You understand, the pain of losing Akim, the shock of finding him. You understand?"

"Yes," says Mrs. Laney, waving away the money. "I also apologize. For my aunt."

"Ax-murderers," says Aunt Lou.

Habril looks up sharply, but Ahim lays a hand on his arm. "We are going now, Mrs. Laney. I thank you for your kindness." He takes the twenty-pound notes from Habril and lays them on the table, anchoring them under the foot of a glass vase.

"Blood money," says Aunt Lou.

"Phone money," says Ahim. "Good-bye, Mrs. Laney, and thank you. *Salullah*, Mary. *Salullah*, Aunt Lou."

"Good-bye," says Mrs. Laney. And then she can't help herself, a gracious beam of blue crosses her brain. "God bless," she adds.

10

Now I have a choice: stay with Mrs. Laney and Mary and Aunt Lou, or go with Ahim and Habril. If Akim was still Ahim, the choice would be easier, but the "h" to "k" has changed him; his face looks harder. Even so, he still pulls me like a magnet. Why? Because he is the only physical link I have with the past, with Aelfin? Or because every time I look at him, I see the future as well as the past, as though he was some kind of gateway through which I have to pass in order to know my own destiny? Maybe it's neither of these, maybe it's just because there are things I still need to know, like why did he do it, why did Ahim press the button on so many lives?

Mrs. Laney accompanies her guests to the front door. Her brain is gentle and has a kind of background sound like the Muzak they play in shopping malls. I don't mean it is that sound, of course (it's more pops and sighs and lah-lahs), but it has that effect, simultaneously soothing and irritating. *Nice men*, she's thinking. *I'm sure they are nice men, really. Bit overwrought; well, you would be, wouldn't you? Good of them to leave the money for the phone. Probably will have to buy a new one. No one mends anything these days. Got to see to Aunt Lou. Poor Aunt Lou.*

Truth is, I'd go mad holed up in Mrs. Laney's brain. As for being inside Aunt Lou's brain for any length of time . . . well, as well as being potentially suicidally drying, it could really loosen a person's grip on reality. I mean, she's crazy; she's not crazy. I once read a true-life story about a woman wrongly committed to a mental asylum who was in there thirty years before she could convince anyone she was sane. The staff knew she'd been committed so assumed she was mad. They saw what they expected to see. Which brings me back (as everything seems to nowadays) to suicide-bombing. We imagine the bombers have lost the plot, that they cannot be normal, rational human beings. But I think Ahim is a normal human being. As normal as any of us are anyway. And I don't like that thought—it's confusing, it's scary.

I slither out of Mrs. Laney's brain and go to hover by Akim. I'm going to call him Akim now; try to get used to this new, supposedly more dangerous man. Mary is also hovering, she can't leave the men alone with her eyes. She's waiting, as if she needs to know something, too. And I remember how she cried out in her sleep, in her dreams. I don't dream anymore (probably because I don't sleep anymore), but in my waking dreams, Mary is there, just like Akim. I realize I am also drawn to her. Is this a para-spirit thing? Have I acquired some magnetic sensitivity along with my new spirit self? Maybe not. Maybe I'm just twitching because I want to go into Mary's brain.

I do.

I'm itching to do it.

I have that sensation you sometimes get when you stand on the edge of an underground train platform and, just for a moment, the danger draws you, you think you'll jump off, just as you hear the train coming. But, of course, you don't jump. And I don't jump, either. I leave Mary alone, just as everyone seems to leave Mary alone. Solitaire. You see, I could hurt her and I don't want to do that. I reckon life hurts Mary plenty enough already.

"Good-bye," says Mrs. Laney. She opens the door and

steers the men out onto the cold, gray landing.

Decision time: No contest, I have to go with Akim. But do I actually have to travel in my murderer's head? No. I could travel with Habril. Idea of genius. Habril's brain is large, his airways open, free-flowing. The journey to the fissure is easy.

"Hello," says a voice as I arrive.

I draw back instantly.

"Oh, there's plenty of room," says the voice, which is soft and welcoming. "I'm Padua. Make yourself at home. Long time since I had a guest."

I make myself as small as I can. "Thanks," I say. "Cassina." My voice doesn't sound soft, it sounds rather choked. I think this is the first time anyone welcomed me anywhere since I became a para-spirit.

"A girl," says Padua. "How wonderful."

"Thirteen years old," I say, unable to keep the mournfulness from my voice. If she's going to mother me, I just might let her for a bit. I've been some places recently, and I feel that way you do when you want someone to take care of you, make you a meal, and wash and iron your clothes. In the absence of a mouth or a body, I'll just make do with the verbal pampering.

"Thirteen," she says. "I'm so sorry. At least I made it to thirty-eight."

"How did you die then?" I ask. Okay, maybe I'm reverting to type, maybe I don't do small and vulnerable very well, or at least not for very long. Even so I don't consider this an intrusive question; in fact, in para-spirit terms, I think it has to rate as small talk. I mean, what else have newly acquainted para-spirits got in common?

"It was a spur of a moment thing," says Padua. "I helped someone, a child, and . . . things didn't turn out quite the way I expected."

Sounds interesting, so I leave a pause, wait for more details. None come.

"It was a long time ago," she adds finally, lamely.

"I was killed by a bomb," I announce jollily.

"Not the station bomb?"

"Exactly that one," I say.

"I'm so sorry," Padua repeats, and then she adds in a slightly indulgent, motherly voice, "Habril and his bombs."

"Habril! I thought it was Akim's bomb."

"Habril's the cell commander. The trainer. He ordered the mission. Akim just carried it out."

"*Just?*" I query.

"Well, no, of course not. Akim carried it out willingly, joyfully. I went with him that day."

"You went with him?" I say. "Are you crazy?" I hear myself use the word *crazy* again, which makes me pause. I'm not sure I know what this word means anymore. I regroup: "Didn't you think you might get blown to kingdom come?"

"Kingdom come," Padua repeats. Her turn for the questions now. "Is that your heaven?"

Tell you the truth, I've never thought about that. "Kingdom come" is just an expression, right? Wrong. I guess it means the kingdom of God, my God. Got to have that discussion with myself about God. Why do I keep putting it off?

"Maybe it is," I say evasively.

"Maybe I wanted to be blown to kingdom come," Padua says. "Or at least to someplace other than here. Maybe I wanted to move on."

I can relate to that. "But you survived."

"Yes."

"Do we always survive, Padua? I mean, can you kill a para-spirit? Do we die? Do we move on, go someplace else? I have to know. Not knowing is killing me."

She gives a little snuffle, which could be a laugh, an affectionate one, or maybe the beginning of a sob. "No one knows. But there are supposed to be ways, only . . ." She trails off.

". . . no one knows what ways."

"Yes."

"Terrific."

A silence.

"Akim survived, too," I offer then. "That must have been a shock."

"No," says Padua. "He was always going to survive."

"What?"

"Akim's an Aeternal."

"I'm sorry?"

"An Aeternal. You can't kill Aeternals. Or, at least you can, but not with bullets, not with bombs."

"Steady on," I say. "You're going way too fast for me."

"Akim was a quite ordinary child, until he was about four, maybe five. His family lived just to the south of Sacrini, by the Southern Gate. They, like many of the villagers, had olive groves there, olives growing in the shadow of the wall. While the adults harvested the crop the kids played. One of the games was Paint the Wall."

"Paint the wall?"

"Yes. I think it was kids near the North Gate who started it. They used to get bits of rag and soak them in paint and then fire them with slingshots at the wall."

"Why?"

"They fired white paintballs, blue, black. The colors of the T'lanni flag. That was the game, to try and create the three stripes of the T'lanni flag on the wall. Most of the paintballs fell short. It wasn't much in the way of defiance."

"And the soldiers in the gun turret—they shot a child for that?"

"That particular day, most of the older boys, they were

helping with the harvest. One particular boy, a handsome lad . . . his mother . . . she would always try and stop him paint-walling. That's what the teenagers called it, paint-walling. 'Why you, Omaz? Why do you have to be the ringleader?' his mother asked. But it did no good. Omaz even got himself a special slingshot, a metal one; all the others had wooden ones. That day Omaz helped with the olives and lent his slingshot to Akim, who was bored with olive-picking."

"The soldiers must have seen how small the kid was?"

"There was an inquiry, of course. There always is. The soldiers said it was the metal. It glinted in the sun. They thought the child had a gun. They were just defending themselves. Returning fire."

I remember the rifle shots and Akim's memory of the little boy with the painty hands. I remember the slow, slow bullet. "Only the bullet didn't actually hit him?"

"The bullet did hit him. The moment after, a woman who'd seen the danger had thrown herself at him, tried to protect him."

I see then the woman from Akim's memory, the shape she made when she flung herself across the boy, and it reminds me of how Akim—Ahim who was—threw himself across Aelfin at the station.

"She kissed him," Padua says slightly dreamily. "The woman kissed him."

"And the bullet dissolved," I say.

"Yes," she says, "how did you know?"

"I've been in his head, too. The bomb made him forget stuff, but he's beginning to remember now. Although I thought the dissolving bullet must just be some muddled memory."

"No. It's true. And also true that the woman saved him. That she made him an Aeternal," says Padua.

"I still don't really get it."

"Nor did he," says Padua. "He saw the bullet dissolve, but he didn't believe it. Even though he was so little, he knew that bullets don't dissolve. So he thought he must be mistaken. He thought the bullet must have hit the woman instead because she was dead, lying beside him dead. So that's what he told them, that an unknown woman had saved him."

"So what really happened?"

"He became an Aeternal, I told you," Padua says sharply.

"And the woman?"

"She died," Padua repeats. "Though not of the bullets. She had no bullet wounds."

Ever have that feeling that someone's not telling you the whole story?

"Why did she do whatever she did, try and save the boy? Was she a relation?"

"No," says Padua.

"A T'lanni then, one of the villagers?"

"Yes, she was a villager there," says Padua. "As I was. Then."

"And she sacrificed herself for the boy?"

"I'm not sure it was a sacrifice," says Padua. "She probably had her reasons."

"What, like altruism?" I say. I wrote a whole paper on altruism for religious education last term (how long ago does *that* seem)—what the world would be like if everyone acted for the benefit of other people, not just for their own benefit. Mr. Carmichael (who's quite acerbic for a scriptures teacher) called it an "interesting fantasy" and asked me to check out Darwin's theory of evolution.

"Altruism!" Padua gives another choky sort of para-spirit laugh.

"Why can't we laugh properly anymore?" I ask then.

"Maybe nothing's funny anymore," she replies.

Right.

"In any case," I say, "how do you know all this stuff about Akim?"

I feel a kind of stiffening as though she's drawing her droplets in, as though I've spoken out of turn. "I know it because . . . because, I've been in his head." Then she adds quickly, "Not that he knew about his change of status, of course, not then. Nor during his teens or his early twenties. Let himself forget. Didn't even know it as he walked into that station with the bomb strapped to his waist."

"He knew he was chosen."

"Chosen. Yes. His mother's words to him. But they were just words. He never knew he was invulnerable. I tell you, when he went into that station, he thought he would die. He thought he'd be a martyr."

But you *knew differently, didn't you, Padua?* I think. *How come?* And then, because I'm in suspicious mode I say, "Hang on a minute. If you were with Akim at the station, how did you get back here to Habril? Habril didn't even know where Akim was until this morning."

She's happy to answer this. "After the explosion, Akim just wandered, dazed. He didn't know who he was, let alone where he should be going. He was still drifting at dusk, only he got lucky, fell upon some soup kitchen. The workers gave him food and found clothes for him. In fact those rather unpleasant ones he's still wearing. They also offered him a place in a night shelter, but he refused. He said he knew where he was going. I didn't believe him, but then he began to head straight toward Habril's road, got right to the door of the shop—the apartment's above a vegetable shop—and then began to walk on by. Habril's window was open, the window of the living room, and I could see him pacing about the room. I had one of those para-spirit moments of madness when you think you can do something, intervene. Have you had that yet, Cassina?"

"Yes." Oh, yes.

"So I floated up to the window, as though I could bang on it, attract Habril's attention, so he'd look down and see Akim."

"But you couldn't and he didn't."

"Yes. By which time Akim had wandered off. So I just floated into the apartment, returned to Habril. He is my main host, you know. Not Akim. Habril's my host."

There's another silence between us in which Habril's brain flashes: *home*. I've been so absorbed in my conversation with Padua I realize I've missed the whole journey from Mrs. Laney's apartment. We seem now to be in some sort of main street, with a small parade of stores: a drugstore, a Co-Op, a betting parlor, a bakery, a newsstand, and yes—a fruit-and-vegetable stand. Habril is striding purposefully toward a blank white door to the right of the stand. The door has two locks, and he undoes both of them before letting himself and Akim into a long dark corridor at the end of which are some uncarpeted stairs. Both men ascend the stairs and meet another double-locked door. Again Habril is swift with the keys, and he holds the door open for Akim. We pass through a small kitchen with old-fashioned appliances and bare blue Formica surfaces, to an equally spartan living room. There's a wooden-armed sofa, two hard, upright chairs, and a black TV and VCR. The wallpaper is dirty cream, with a slightly raised squarish pattern on it. Above the gas fireplace, where someone else might have hung a picture, or a mirror, Habril and Akim have pinned a series of little pencil-written notes:

I believe in Ingali, who smote the desert with the Word of God.
I believe in the destiny of my own deeds, that whatsoever I do

well in this life will do well for me in the afterlife and whatso-
ever I do ill will go ill for me in the afterlife.
And God said call others to the way of our Lord.
Repel evil wheresoever you shall find it.
Anatarah istali batak. My God, the One, the Only.
And J'lal said, "Ingali, bring me the souls of the martyrs, for
them I love, they shall be with me in Paradise forever."

Padua, seeing me look, says: "Verses from the scroll of
the Holy Desert." Her voice sounds thinner than it did,
drier, and I know I'm overstaying my welcome because I
am also feeling a little parched at the edges.

"I should go," I say.

"But come back," she says. "Please come back."

I'm floating out of Habril's head, thinking about loneliness, when I see the newspaper. It's lying on the floor
with a pile of other newspapers; it has the crumpled, crin-
kled look of a well-read paper, one that's at least a week
old. The simple banner headline reads: "Bomb Dead,"
underneath which are about fifteen head-and-shoulder
shots of men, women, and children. On the bottom line,
there's a picture of me, and there's a picture of Aelfin.

Of course, despite needing to get into Akim's head fast,
I'm straight down to read what the captions are. Under
Aelfin's picture it says, "Aelfin Dixon, gold-medal gymnast."
Under mine it says, "Cassina Dixon, aged 13."

So that's that then.

I retreat to Akim's head, go straight to the fissure, and
grind my nonexistent teeth.

Akim has seen the newspaper, too. He picks it up, scans
the pictures, stops at Aelfin's.

"Aelfin," he says, trying the name in his mouth. And I
realize he hasn't known her name until now. "Aelfin Dixon."

"And Cassina," I mention, but he doesn't.

He focuses on Aelfin, and her features begin to dissolve

slightly; she becomes Mary and then his brain begins to pull again, the way it does when he thinks about Esta. But no more pictures come.

"I did it," he says to Habril. "I killed them."

"Yes," says Habril. "*Antab batak.* The Holy One is Lord."

"Why did I do it?" asks Akim.

Habril stares at him. "You don't know? You don't remember?"

Akim shakes his head.

Habril goes to the TV set and selects one of the four videos that are neatly stacked beside it. He turns on the television set and pushes the video into the slot.

"Sit," says Habril.

Akim chooses one of the hard chairs and sits.

The television springs to life. The picture is of Akim. He is sitting on the same hard chair, only behind him, painted on a sheet, is a huge spread of wings. Inked in black where the head of this "angel" might be are the words: "Rapat is the duty of every T'lanni." Propped up against the angel wings are two rifles. I'm not exactly a firearms expert, but they look like those Kalashnikovs you see slung around the necks of Chechen rebels.

Akim salutes the camera. He looks wide-eyed and under-slept.

"Tomorrow I will be a martyr," he declares. "Only the believers know what this means. This is my free decision. I urge you all to follow me to the paths of Paradise. God is good. *Antab batak.* All martyrdom operations, if done for Holy Rapat, hurt less than a gnat's bite."

He then flings himself to the floor and begins prayers and exhortations in a language I don't understand, though I can pick out some words: *Ingali, Rapat, J'lal, Hakamdaba.* During the fifteen minutes or so that the video lasts, Akim's brain is on fire, different lobes cracking with recognition, responding as if the words are triggers and his brain the gun. But the word that causes the largest explosion is *salanika*. With this word come pictures and, of course, despite the danger, I crawl out of the fissure to try and see those pictures, to try and understand. We are in a large rectangular room, its whitewashed walls neatly etched with verses from the Holy Desert Words. Hundreds of verses, thousands maybe; the walls are almost black with them. On the ceiling is a huge painting of Ingali, his wings outstretched as if to gather up everyone in the room. There are no chairs in the room, no furniture at all, in fact, only a scattering of white cushions on the floor. Men and women, but mainly men, sit together. In unison they pray; they hold their hearts, they kiss their rings.

At the door is a newcomer. It's Akim; he looks young, frightened, and in the wrong place. An older man stands up; it's Habril.

"Welcome, brother," he says. *"Salanika."* He takes Akim by the shoulder, steers him toward the group. "This is Akim," he says, "whom God has brought to this House of J'lal."

All those in the room stand.

"We welcome you," they cry. "Brother in faith, brother in God, brother of ours. *Salanika.*" Each of them puts his ringed hand to his heart.

Akim puts his own hand to his chest and then he begins to cry.

In Habril's bleak apartment, Akim shakes his head, as if to try and dispel this memory. The screens in his head fuzz, and I return to the fissure.

The video is ending, a voice off camera saying, "May God be with you, may God give you success so that you achieve Paradise." Akim is lying prone in front of the guns. From his position on the floor, he replies, *"Antab batak.* We will meet in Paradise."

Habril switches off the tape; he smiles.

But the memories aroused by the video are not switched

off so easily. *Salanika*, says Akim's brain. *Salanika. Brother.* The words radiate a kind of warmth so that even I, in the fissure, feel the touch of an angel wing, like someone was caring for me, enfolding me. Again Akim tries to shake them away. I feel him struggle with himself as he finally says, "It's not an answer."

Habril's smile dies. "What?" he says.

"It doesn't answer why," Akim repeats.

"You know why," says Habril. "You trained for months. We trained you. I trained you. Have you forgotten the Holy Desert Words? Each of us is enjoined by God to bring the world to His paths. To fight the unbelievers. For their own sakes, Akim, so they may also know God and enter Paradise. And to reclaim Sacrini, such as God gave to the T'lannis and the T'lannis alone. *Antab batak*. And to encourage the minds of mankind to return to the holy purpose, to look to our souls and not our possessions. Nothing we possess will come with us to Paradise, only our deeds which alone will speak for us in front of J'lal, the Holy, the Only. This is the Holy Path, and God blesses those who tread His Journey. Akim, my brother, my friend, you know this in your heart. God chose you to be a martyr, to join him in Paradise."

"Only I didn't die. I didn't join him in Paradise. Why's that, Habril?"

"God is good. God worked His miracle. That we should all see and know him. You are God's miracle, Akim."

In Akim's brain a bullet dissolves, a car door slams.

"Did I have a daughter, Habril?" asks Akim suddenly.

"No," says Habril. "No. You know the rules. T'lannis do not take fathers for martyrs. Fathers have other duties."

"I think I have a daughter," says Akim. "Had a daughter?" The pictures of Aelfin and Mary come, the picture of the girl with no face.

"No," says Habril. "No daughter."

Akim looks at the newspaper, at the picture of Aelfin. "I killed daughters," he says.

"Yes," says Habril. "And you will again."

"No," says Akim.

"God has saved you. *Antab batak*. Chosen you for a new mission."

Chosen, chosen.

"It is your sacred duty."

"No. Never!"

Habril reaches his hand inside his jacket, pulls out a small black-barreled handgun with the long nose of a silencer. He puts it close to Akim, on the hard chair beside him. "This is a war, Akim. God's war."

Akim stands up.

"No," says my murderer.

Habril spins the gun, watches it twirl. "Maybe next time you will be lucky," he says. "Maybe next time God will take you for a martyr."

Akim also looks at the gun.

"I had a child," he says.

"No," says Habril.

"Yes," says Akim, and he's not so calm now, there's a fierce red anger zigzagging his brain. "A daughter."

"No."

"Esta." And for the first time when he says her name, there is no picture of Aelfin, no picture of Mary, no faceless desert dancer. The red anger combusts, it explodes into a huge, tactile, moving face which smiles and laughs in every part of Akim's brain. Esta with a million dark, searching eyes and a mouth with parted lips, revealing tiny, pearly baby teeth. Esta with a little snub nose and olive skin and happiness dimpled up in her cheeks. "Dada," she says.

Akim picks up the gun.

"No," says Habril. "Are you crazy?"

"Yes," says Akim. Esta lies in the no-man's-land dirt, her face upturned to the sun, a tiny dribble of blood coming from between her baby teeth. "Crazy."

Habril begins to back away. But it is to his own temple that Akim puts the gun. I can't see it, but he pushes it so hard against his skull, it's like he's jabbing it into me.

I'm out of his brain like a bat out of hell. All my brave talk of "moving on" and "fulfilling my destiny" is right out of the window. I'd be out of the window, too, if there was an open one anywhere near. As it is, I just fly up to the ceiling, breaking all known para-spirit records for speedy retreats, and I hover right in the farthest-away-from-the-action corner.

"God forgive me," Akim says and, with the gun still to his own head, he pulls the trigger.

There's a whoomph sound, like someone punching a cushion, and Habril falls to the ground.

Akim remains standing, a small ring of gunpowder at his temple.

A moment later Habril pulls himself up from his own shock, stares at the figure in front of him. "Holy Lord," he cries. "Holy, Holy Lord. I know you now. God makes you plain. You are the boy from Sacrini, from the Southern Gate. The boy they said that bullets couldn't kill."

He prostrates himself, squashes his face to the floor.

"I was there that day. I was there! But, God forgive me, I never believed it. But it's true. Praise J'lal; praise the Holy One. You are His miracle."

Akim touches his temple where the bullet kissed him, looks at the smudge of black on his finger. Then he sits and puts his head in his hands.

Habril brings himself back to his feet. "You must see God's purpose now, *antab batak*," he says urgently. "You must fulfill your destiny for God. The whole world awaits you, Akim Watabi. Think of what you could do—what we could do together. People will see you, Akim, and they will believe. The whole world at your feet—at God's feet."

"There is nothing," Akim says wearily, "you can do to make me kill another child."

"For the good of the world, Akim, to show God's power in action. You are the chosen one, Akim, it is written for you."

"No. Don't speak of it again."

There's a pause and then Habril says softly, "Don't underestimate me, brother." His face is hard and still. "Besides, if you are the child from the Southern Gate, I think you'll find you owe me."

11

It's in the night that Padua comes. I don't see her coming, of course, because—at last—Akim is asleep, his eyelids shut fast. But I do feel her—or feel something—a presence in Akim's airways, the pressure of something driving toward the fissure, a push of air, and me being forced back, jostled, invaded. And for the first time I have sympathy with Mac and Blacoe, it's quite a frightening experience being on the receiving end of a visiting para-spirit.

"Sorry," she says, realigning herself and trying to take up less space. "Were you dozing?"

"Sure," I say, a little on the back foot, or back droplet. "After the evening we had?"

"Sorry," she says, "me, neither."

There's something fluttery about her, she can't keep still, each of her droplets seems to be beating, but separately, like she was a hundred restless hearts.

"What's up?" I say.

"Nothing," she says quickly. And then, "How's Akim? How's he been?"

"Pretty good for someone who tried to shoot himself in the head." This is a lie. Akim has been crying, sobbing like a baby. I've had three uninterrupted, exhausting hours of it, and I'm in no mood to make it the subject of a discussion.

"I'm pleased," says Padua. "I thought he wouldn't be able to bear it."

"Bear what exactly?"

"Knowing. Having it confirmed that he was an Aeternal."

"Oh that!" I wish I could laugh. Akim the chosen one. "You don't think surviving the suicide bomb might have given him the tip-off?"

"It's not the same, there's knowing and knowing. Knowing with your head is not the same as knowing with your heart." The restlessness is more of a shudder now. "That you're immortal. That you can't die. Can't be killed anyway."

"You sound like you're talking from personal experience."

"Me? How could I be?" she says abruptly. "I'm a para-spirit."

The full stop is like a slap. I shut up but only for a moment. "Could you stop jigging about?"

"Sorry," she says and shrinks slightly farther away, which, of course, makes me feel bad.

"He was upset about his daughter," I concede then. "Or at least that's what I thought he was upset about. Not the Aeternal thing but Esta. His brain was full of Esta. She is his daughter, isn't she?"

"Was his daughter. She was killed at a checkpoint in Sacrini almost three years ago now."

I remember Akim's dream of the car driving toward the mirage city, the old woman in black, the young woman in Western clothes, the little girl in the backseat. This I am interested in discussing. "What exactly happened?"

"They were going to the hospital. Manina, Esta's mother, was driving, taking the old woman, the grandmother, for a checkup, she had problems with her legs. The checkpoint soldiers were jittery, very jittery. They'd had information about a possible suicide bomber. At first, when the soldiers saw the car was full of women, they let it go. But that's when the call came. A 'woman in black,' that was the information; the suspect would be wearing women's clothes, or even be a woman. They couldn't take any chances."

"So they shot them all?"

"Fear. It makes you panic." Padua's droplets are drumming. "The grandmother—she survived. Manina was critically injured. She lived ten days but did not regain consciousness. She died of her wounds in the hospital to which they were taking the grandmother." I feel Padua pause, try to control her droplets.

"And then?"

"Akim was mad with grief. Mad. He'd lost his wife, he'd lost his child. He was young, only twenty-four, committed, idealistic, and torn apart. He said if they suspected suicide bombers, that's what they'd get. He'd be what they'd accused his wife and child of being. He'd be the bomber. What had he got to lose?"

"Besides, he was chosen."

"Yes, perhaps at that stage there was something of destiny in it. The destiny he'd been resisting all those years, when he tried to live an ordinary life."

"But why England? Why did he come here?"

"He didn't want to come to England; offered himself at once to a cell in his hometown, but they laughed at him. Told him personal revenge was not acceptable to God. He needed to cleanse himself of all personal thoughts. The war being waged was a military one, not the result of personal bitterness. That's when he came to London. Lay low. Joined a House of J'lal where no one knew him. Bided his time."

"And met Habril. Only Habril didn't recognize him?"

"Akim was only five during the Southern Gate incident. Habril must have been a decade older. He'd changed continents. Changed names. In fact they'd both changed names.

Besides, Akim knew what he wanted. He was clever, clever and silent. He never spoke of the homeland. Never spoke of Manina. Of Esta. He made himself forget them. I was in his head sometimes then. He joined the brotherhood. Took them as his family, let them hold his hand, be his life. In time he had something new to live for."

"Or die for," I say sourly. And then: "But it was different after the bomb? Is that what you"re saying? When he forgot who he was, but not who his family were?"

"Yes." At last Padua is still.

"Why do you like him so much?" I ask then.

"I'm sorry?"

"Akim, why do you care for him? I mean, you tell that story as though it explains things, as though it justifies him blowing up innocent people."

"Innocent," she repeats. "What makes you think the people he killed were innocent?"

I don't believe this. "Because I was one of them!" I splutter. "Remember!"

"You mean because bad things happen on the other side of the world, they don't concern you? You're not responsible?"

"Of course not, how was anything that happened to Akim's family my fault?"

"Well, I think," says Padua, "maybe if one person suffers anywhere in the world, we all have blood on our hands."

"Yeah, but not quite as much blood as Akim has on his!" How come she's twisting everything? "I mean, some things have to be wrong, don't they, Padua? You know, like in right and wrong? Like it was wrong of Hitler to try and exterminate the Jews. No special pleading—just plain wrong. Well, blowing people up—that has to be in the same category. Plain old wrong."

"And wrong of those who shot Akim's wife and child," she says softly.

"Yes. Sure. Of course." And I'm just about to add, quoting my mother, "And when did two wrongs make a right?" when I remember how I strung myself about Akim's heart, tried to crush the breath from him as he crushed it from me on the station concourse. So I keep quiet.

"Besides, it's not easy being an Aeternal," Padua says suddenly. "You have to live with stuff, live with it a long time."

"What's that got to do with anything? You said he didn't even know he was an Aeternal when he waltzed into that station and detonated my life!"

"He'll be sorry. He'll have a long time to be sorry."

"Great. That really makes a difference." It seems grubby to make this so personal, but—for me—it is personal.

There's a silence during which she begins to jig about again.

"Come on, Padua," I say, "I may not have been your bosom pal for a million years, but last time we met you didn't twitch. What's with the twitching?"

"Habril," she responds finally. "I know him. He's going to do something bad."

"Like what exactly?"

"I don't know. But with a girl. A girl called Mary."

"Mary? Mary Laney?"

"You know her?"

"Of course. And so do you," I say, hearing a little sharpness in my voice. "You saw her when you came with Habril to get Akim. Mrs. Laney's child. The kid with the mousy hair and the big eyes and the Mickey Mouse ring?"

"Oh, Mary," says Padua.

"So—what's he going to do, what's the plan?"

"I don't know."

"You must know. You've been holed up in Habril's head all evening. Had access to all his thoughts. Don't you pay attention?" What am I getting so worked up about? What's Mary to do with me?

"I don't know, Cassina. I really don't. I just know he's going there. Tomorrow morning. He's going back to the apartment."

"Then I'm going with him," I say. "You can stay with your beloved Akim. I'm going with Habril."

"Okay," she says meekly.

Her capitulation is so immediate that it occurs to me that maybe this is what she has wanted all along, to come back to Akim, to spend some time in his fissure. Habril may be her main host, but it's clear she likes to swap about. I think she's missing Akim. So even if there wasn't the looming problem of both of us drying out if we spend much more time together, I'm going. I've had enough of her.

"Right," I say. "I'm off."

"Good luck," she says.

Yeah, right.

I float across Akim's bedroom toward the door, making for the keyhole, imagining this is the way Padua has come. But the keyhole is blocked, the key wedged in from the other side. Habril has locked Akim in! So much for trust. But doors do not pose a problem for me, at least not this ill-fitting one; about a hundred para-spirits could fit between the ill-sawed door and the warped doorframe. I slip into the hall. There is only one other shut door: Habril's bedroom, I presume. This time I do go through the keyhole. I've always wanted to go through a keyhole, ever since I saw a ghost doing it in a movie when I was about five. I have to say the experience is not monumental, it's like being in a very short, very dull, metal tunnel. Of course you can see bits of the lock mechanism, which is interesting if you're that way inclined; which, I discover, I'm not.

Habril's bedroom is as sparse as Akim's—no privileges for cell commanders then. He has the same hard-looking slatted bed frame with an identically thin mattress. His white sheets are tucked beneath a meager cream wool blanket, and his bedspread is a too-small piece of red cloth. The cloth is lightly sewn in gold and beautiful, but so frayed and so much the wrong shape for the bed, I wonder if he and Akim—who has an almost identical piece of red cloth—started with one large cover and decided to cut it in half. Habril's clothes, which are laid neatly over an upright chair, are the only personal items in the room. There are no ornaments, no pictures, no photos, no trinkets of any sort. It reminds me of Mrs. Laney's toyless sitting room. Nothing there to indicate the presence of a child. Nothing here to betray what sort of man Habril is, to reveal what might go on in his mind.

Heating is not a priority in this apartment, but Habril is without pajamas, or without a pajama top anyway. He is lying with his slight arms nakedly tucked around his shoulders, as though he is hugging himself. I know I'm only peering in the half light, but he doesn't look so harsh anymore. Asleep, his face has softened: the hard, passionate lines of the day smoothing out into something more gentle, tranquil. He looks almost girlish, beautiful even. I hover there for some long moments, just gazing. Does sleep do this to everyone, I wonder: take away our cares, make us more lovely?

Next to Habril's pillow is a copy of the scroll of the Holy Desert Words. Two golden clips hold it open at a particular place. I float across to see what verses Habril has been studying. "Pardon your fellow man, even as you wish God to pardon you," I read. "Overlook faults, let quietness come after anger. Forgive that you may be forgiven."

All of a sudden I don't feel quite so tender toward him. Habril didn't forgive me much! Me with my full Western stomach and my empty soul. Did I have an empty soul? I don't think so. I think I loved people and they loved me back. Especially my mother. I think I loved the earth. I'm sure I did. Looked up at the sky—appreciated it. Thought of things bigger than myself. Didn't I? Didn't I? And in any case, what if I was empty? What if I was the emptiest-headed, most hollow-souled body on the block, what business of Habril's was it exactly?

His breath flutters, and he turns toward me a little, which I choose to interpret as an invitation and so allow myself to ascend his airways. I have a sudden panic that some interloping para-spirit may have invaded Habril's fissure, but I find it empty. Despite his peaceful face, I half expect that Habril's brain will be zapping with dreams, but no, there is only a calm heaviness here and a kind of blanketing color, a very pale violet-brown. For the few hours before dawn, I almost rest.

When Habril wakes (and he does so at six-forty-five precisely, without an alarm) he arises immediately. I imagine his thoughts will turn at once to the day ahead, to what he has in store for Mary, but his mind is on prayer: *Anatarah istali batak, Holy J'lal, the One, the Only God.* The words come not with hard flashes but with a kind of gentle gladness. He goes to the bathroom and begins his ablutions. As he recites the ring prayers, something strange and rather beautiful happens in his brain. It's difficult to describe, but everything seems to become lighter somehow; the colors of him, his emotions, they begin to glow both pale and bright, so that even in my fissure I experience his sense of expansion, as if he is nurturing the seed of himself. The prayers refresh him, purify him but also seem to make him grow. He fills up with the brightness, grows wider, deeper, more uplifted so that, with the last kiss, he seems to be, even in my dark fissure, fountaining light: *Anatarah istali batak.*

He returns to his bedroom and opens a built-in corner

cupboard that I didn't notice before. The shelves are densely packed with shoes, jackets, hats, glasses. Habril selects a pair of jeans, a white T-shirt, a thick red baseball jacket, and a baseball cap which he puts on his head back to front, adjusting the angle by looking in the mirror screwed to the inside of the cupboard door. He tucks his dark hair under the cap.

Disguise, his brain hums happily as, from his memory lobes, he pulls the picture of himself as the suicide-bomb suspect, the one from the newspaper that Aunt Lou thrust in front of him.

He adds a pair of wraparound sunglasses; then his brain synapses *December*, and he takes them off again. He substitutes a pair of steel-rimmed spectacles and turns again to observe his Westernized reflection. He smiles. Is it his jolliness that makes me afraid? Maybe. Maybe it's also the fact that inside the jacket there's a deep pocket and into that pocket he puts the black handgun.

In the kitchen he makes himself a glass of mint tea and cuts himself a thin slice of melon. He scribbles a note for Akim (the "Akim" is underlined twice) and leaves it propped up on the kitchen table, between the salt and the pepper. Most of the note is in his own language, but he signs it "Back soon, Habril," as if he was just popping out for a pint of milk. When he's eaten and drunk, he goes to Akim's room and, very softly, unlocks the door. Akim is peacefully asleep, his body lying open, relaxed. He looks as if he doesn't have a care in the world. Habril stares at him and then makes a silent bow, the sort you might make at an altar. "Open his eyes," Habril begins, and I realize he's praying at the shrine of Akim. "Holy J'lal, let your warrior see your cause. Let him go forth and smite the hearts of the unbelievers with your words as you once smote the desert. Let his blind eyes see what is clearer than the day. That he is your chosen one. Holy, holy Lord."

Returning to his own room, Habril selects a pair of black gloves and pulls them over his hands, covering the three rings on the middle finger of his left hand. Then he leaves the apartment, double-locking the door behind him. He descends the stairs and lets himself onto the street, double-locking the street door also. He tests this door, pushing at it to check it is secure. Until he sees the light, beloved Akim, it seems, is not to escape.

The fruit-and-vegetable stand man is already at work, unloading brussels sprouts from a van. He looks up as Habril exits, as if he would greet him, but seeing the baseball cap and jacket, turns away again.

Excellent, acknowledges Habril's brain.

Habril begins to walk along the street, turns his face up to the sky. It's a perfect English December day, crisp and bright and blue.

Happy, says Habril's brain. And, just for one moment, I think, maybe Padua's wrong, maybe Habril has no bad intentions this morning at all: gun or no gun, how can a man have evil in his heart and be so happy? Besides, there is still nothing in his brain about plans, nothing in his brain about Mary, there's just a sense of calm and hopefulness.

He's not a big man, Habril, but he strides along, his steps made bigger by their purposefulness. It's early still but the market street bustles with workers, with deliveries, with the slam of crates on pavements while, inside the stores, shelves are being stacked and cash registers pinged to life. It's nearly Christmas, so there's tinsel in the windows, a snowman in the drugstore, a gold foil Season's Greetings in the newsstand.

Habril sees none of this. He's concentrating on the movement of his body, the pleasant feeling of going forward. The pictures in his head are unlike any I've seen before: they're abstract; the colors warm, red, yellow, orange, white, the colors I used to see when I was alive and closed my eyelids and looked at the sun. The images swim and pulse, and gradually I realize the pulses are in time with his stride. After about five minutes, when he begins to slow a little, the abstract pictures take on deeper colors, sharper edges; a pavement arrives and then a building; the street begins to take unhurried shape. And yet Habril still does not see what I see.

The more the road appears, the stores, the bustle, the clearer it becomes that he does not see the people. They remain shadows to him. They wear coats, or hats, or shoes, and they move around; but they are indistinct, their faces flat and featureless. The flower shop delivery man wears the same blurred countenance that a woman with the briefcase on her way to work does: the druggist might be the baker; the baker, the man selling newspapers. At first, I think maybe Habril's just not concentrating fully yet, that he hasn't pulled his mind from hazy, in the same way that, when I had human eyes, I could let them relax, so things fuzzed at the edges. Then we pass a small man with olive skin, a sharp mouth, and surprising, smiling eyes, and Habril sees him, sees him perfectly. I imagine maybe this man is a friend, someone Habril's mind has picked out from the featureless crowd, someone with whom he wishes to interact. But the two men pass on by; they are strangers, except that this man also wears three rings on the middle finger of his left hand. I feel a little clench inside: can it be that Habril only sees T'lannis? That all Western people look alike to him? No, surely not. But time and time again we pass blank-faced Westerners only to see the occasional, perfectly rendered T'lanni.

Not that Habril is paying attention to any of the people around him; in fact the only time his brain really engages is when a gust of wind lifts an empty plastic bag from the gutter and swirls it in front of him. He watches it dance. His brain laughs, infectious flashes of joy leap from lobe to lobe: he loves the plastic bag, its swoops and dives, it entrances him! He knows it's only a bag, a piece of rubbish which should be cleared away, but his brain makes it a bird, fast as a swallow, white as a swan; it dips and curls, his bag, his beautiful, flying, December bag. He laughs out loud, Habril, who kills for a living.

If I'd thought about Habril's brain in advance, which I confess I didn't, I would have imagined it to be like Mac's, like the angry, booted man in the park with his lathered-up look and flared nostrils, lobes primed for red, fizz-cracking anger. Yet here is Habril: soft, vacant, happy. What can explain this? Surely a man who cares passionately about the justness of his cause, a man who's prepared to kill for what he believes in, surely such a man needs a busier, angrier brain than Habril's? I try to think back to my first time with him, the journey from the Laneys' last night. Of course, I was occupied with Padua, giving her all my attention, but if there had been any major fizz-cracking, I would have known, I would have felt it. So there must have been nothing; traveling back home with Akim, a man Habril thought was dead, Habril was quite calm. Is this belief? Is this what it feels like to be sure of yourself, to know with complete conviction that God walks with you?

The bag blows away, but not my uneasiness. Habril turns off the market street and walks down a small residential road until he comes to a modest light blue car: a Vauxhall, I think. It's old and boxy-looking and rusty. Habril climbs in and starts the engine. I want to be driving anywhere except to the Laneys'; but in less than ten minutes, we arrive at the apartment building.

Rapat is the duty of every T'lanni. Even this isn't a flash. It's a mellow wave which billows over all parts of Habril's brain.

He parks, makes his way to the ground-floor entrance, and presses the intercom button. There's a pause, and then a light, childish voice comes over the intercom.

"Hello?" It's Mary.

"Hello," says Habril evenly, in a voice which sounds not at all like his own. "Hello, Mary Laney. It's Father Christmas for you."

There's a pause, followed by something that might be a snuffle or even a giggle and then the sound of the entry-phone buzz. Habril Fazheen is in.

The elevator is on the ground floor already, so Habril gets in and presses for the fourth floor. He steps out onto the concrete landing and rings the bell of Mrs. Laney's apartment.

"Don't do it, Mary!" I want to shout. "Don't open the door!"

The door opens. It's Aunt Lou.

But that's not what Habril sees. Habril sees a largish purple shape with a plate-flat beige face. To tell the truth, Aunt Lou's face powder is excessive this morning, even for her.

"Hello," says Habril. "My name is Omaz Lamyar."

The beige plate tilts. "No, it's not," says Aunt Lou. "Your name is Habril Fazheen."

Go, Aunt Lou!

Habril focuses, and gradually the beige plate gains a pair of violet eyes.

"Is Mrs. Laney in?" he inquires as though her discovering his identity was no challenge at all, as though the conversation was going exactly to plan. He looks over Aunt Lou's shoulder into the apartment.

Mrs. Laney is nowhere to be seen, but we both see Mary. I see a child with a glowing face up a ladder, attempting to put a silver angel with a white net skirt right at the top of an otherwise bare six-foot Christmas tree. Habril sees a multicolored (Mary is wearing purple trousers and a scarlet fleece) blob with a blurred face and no tree at all. I check this. It's true. Habril does not see the tree. In its place he sees a neon flash: buy your trees here, exchange your filthy money for trash, for baubles, buy, buy, buy, buy. . . .

But I see the tree, the tree is all the trees of my childhood rolled into one. It's a blue spruce, I can almost smell it. Why can't para-spirits smell? I want to smell that tree, envelop myself in the scent of all our Christmases, mine and Aelfin's and Mom's and Dad's and Bonnie's. How we would go as a family to choose the perfect tree, Mom eager, Dad embarrassed (Mom had to have *the* perfect tree), Aelfin excited, Bonnie excited, me—pretty grown-up, but hey, it's Christmas, grown-ups can be excited about Christmas, can't they? And yes, of course, Dad would give the money, quite a lot of money. But the money wasn't it—it was carrying the tree home together, Dad in the middle, me on the trunk, Aelfin with the tip spiking in her hair. Mom standing by, proud and smiling, Bonnie lolloping beside us, oblivious. And then, of course, the decorating, every one of those ornaments, those glittering memories being unwrapped again.

Is that how it happened yesterday for the Laneys? Mrs. Laney saying, "Well, after the drama of the morning, I think we better go and choose a tree, don't you?" And them all, even Aunt Lou, putting on hats and coats and taking Bister and choosing a tree.

How will my mother and my father choose a tree this year? I imagine my mother walking toward the pub—we get our tree (*got* our tree) from the man in the pub parking lot—and being unable to go on. But also being unable to walk on by. I imagine her standing there, watching other families buy trees and take them away in net bags, Christmas about to begin. I imagine my father saying: "Come on, Sarah, no point standing here." And my mother just bursting into tears.

"Hello," says Mary, addressing Habril from the ladder. "You said you were Father Christmas."

"Ax-murderer," says Aunt Lou, and she begins to shut the door.

Habril is quick with his foot; a small push, and he's inside the apartment.

"I beg your pardon!" says Aunt Lou.

"Mary," says Habril, "you are needed for a sacred mission." In his brain I'm subject to a burst of transcendental light: *Anatarah istali batak.*

"Don't be ridiculous," says Aunt Lou. She moves at once to the foot of the ladder. "Leave the apartment, now."

Mary comes down a rung on the ladder, puts her little body behind Aunt Lou's larger one. I see a small wild-animal panic in her eyes. Habril can't even see her face. Without haste he shuts the door of the apartment and advances into the living room.

"I said—leave," says Aunt Lou.

Habril swiftly observes the layout of the apartment, swings me left and right as he checks which doors are open and which are closed.

"Is Mrs. Laney here?" Habril asks.

"Yes," says Aunt Lou.

"Mommy," says Mary. "I want Mommy."

"She's out, isn't she?" says Habril.

"No," says Aunt Lou.

"Yes," wails Mary.

"Out with the *dog*," concedes Aunt Lou. She lays emphasis on the word *dog* as though Bister really is a rottweiler—a huge, eager-toothed Cerberus just waiting to sink his fangs into passing intruders. "She'll—they'll—be back any minute."

"Good," says Habril. "Come with me, Mary."

Mary grabs on to Aunt Lou's upper right arm. I see the white grip of her little fingers.

"Over my dead body," says Aunt Lou.

"Fine," says Habril and takes out the gun.

Mary breathes in too quickly and makes a high, hiccupy sound.

"What do you want her for?" asks Aunt Lou. "What are you after?"

"I told you. I need her for a sacred mission. Come, Mary. I'm not going to hurt you." Now he does look up at her, the part of her head that is still visible around Aunt Lou's shoulder. He sees the edge of her mouth; he believes she is smiling.

"You're crazy," observes Aunt Lou. "You're evil. I'm going to call the police."

Habril walks over to the dining table and picks up the phone which, only yesterday, he ripped from the wall. He hands it to Aunt Lou. It has no wire in the back. He smiles, shrugs.

"You're crazy and you're evil and you're going to go to hell," Aunt Lou elaborates.

"I'm going to go to Paradise," says Habril. "And the whole world with me," he adds almost as an afterthought. *"Antab batak."* He holds out his hand. "Come, Mary."

Mary doesn't move.

"It's kidnapping," says Aunt Lou.

"It's important," says Habril.

"There are laws against kidnapping," says Aunt Lou.

"There are laws against many things," says Habril. "Not all of them just."

"I'm not going," says a muffled voice which seems to be coming from inside Aunt Lou's cardigan.

"Course you're not," says Aunt Lou.

Habril raises the gun a little. "Mary . . .," he says and his voice is not so gentle now. Though the inside of his head is still quite mellow.

"Take me," says Aunt Lou suddenly. "Don't take the child. Whatever you want, I'll do it."

Wash my mouth out with soap if I ever spoke ill of the woman. Aunt Lou, my heroine.

"You!" Habril laughs out loud but he also looks. Stares at her until he sees more than the beige plate and the violet eyes. His mind etches in dark eyebrows and a pair of painted lips. "I don't think so," he says, and he advances.

That's when Aunt Lou throws the phone at him. It's heavy and it's old-fashioned and it clips him on the side of the head. Now there is a flash in Habril's head: *Fal'kakka!* his head bawls, and I'm not sure I need a translation. Habril's right arm is swift; he belts Aunt Lou across the face with the barrel of the gun. There's an astonished pause and then Aunt Lou falls to the floor, with the unbending crash of a sawed tree. Mary, exposed on the ladder, screams.

Habril puts his left hand over her mouth and his right hand into his pocket where he deposits the gun. "I'm not going to hurt you," he says again. "Look, I've put the gun away. But you need to be quiet. Do you understand?"

Mary, her eyes like saucers, understands.

Habril takes away his hand.

Mary doesn't make a sound. I want to scream.

"Good," says Habril and lifts Mary to the floor. Both her hands are trembling.

"Come now."

He leads her out of the apartment and into the elevator. "I have a car," he says. "If you make a noise, I'll put you in the trunk. If you're quiet, you travel in the car. Do you understand?"

Mary nods. She looks so frightened I think she may have lost the power of speech.

"Good," says Habril again.

She travels back to Habril's apartment in the front seat

of the car, quiet as a lamb. In her lap, clutched in tight hands, is the silver angel with the white net skirt.

Habril's brain is violet-brown and humming happily. As for me, I have never felt so useless in all of my life.

12

We pull up right in front of the fruit-and-vegetable stand. Habril gets out of the car and goes around to the passenger side and opens the door for Mary. She stumbles out onto the pavement, her limbs thin and disjointed. Habril steers her toward the street door and deals with the locks. A small push, and she's in the dark corridor. He marches her up the steps to the second locked door and twists the keys. In the kitchen of the apartment, he calls out, "Akim, Akim, I have something for you, a gift!"

We arrive in the living room. Akim is sitting on the hard sofa.

"Look!" Habril's brain synapses joy, the joy of the wonderful, floating plastic bag. "For you." Mary has come to a stop. Beneath Habril's right hand, which is hard down on her shoulder, Mary stands like a white post.

"Mary!" Akim exclaims and immediately rises to his feet. "Mary—what on earth . . . ?" He turns on Habril. "What are you playing at, Habril? Why bring Mary here?"

Habril shrugs, laughs. "Persuasion, maybe." He releases Mary, moving across the room to stand by the mantelpiece next to the handwritten words of God. Mary remains exactly where she is, as though his hand was still there, holding her down. "Help you see sense," Habril continues. "Accept your destiny." He pauses. "Pay your dues."

"Mary," Akim says and he moves toward her. She startles, a deer caught in headlights, her body remaining rooted to the ground, but a wild flinch in her eyes, as though she expects to be struck. "Mary, it's okay. I'm not going to hurt you. Habril's not going to hurt you." Akim extends a hand. I see her clench, move enough to turn a tiny shoulder against him.

"Listen to Akim, Mary," Habril says, and he takes the gun from his jacket pocket. "Listen carefully to Akim Watabi. He holds your life in the palm of his hand." He blows lightly down the gun's silencer. "As once his own life was held in the balance."

"Put the gun away, Habril."

"In time," says Habril, and he raises the gun and levels it at Akim's chest. "Now, Mary, do you believe in God?"

Mary gulps.

"Mary?"

"Leave her alone, Habril."

"My mother believes in God," says Mary quickly. "My mother says Christ died for us all."

"But what about you, Mary?"

"My father says . . . Daddy says . . ."

"I'm not asking about your mother, Mary, or about your father. I'm asking about you. What do you believe, Mary?" Habril cocks his head, waits for an answer and, when no answer comes, he pulls the trigger.

There's the whoomphing cushion noise. Mary's hand barely gets to her mouth before the bullet reaches Akim's breast. I watch her eyes as she watches the bullet dissolve against his Salvation Army shirt. One second the bullet is there, hard and brassy and swift, and the next it simply melts away, leaving the smallest of sooty rings on the pocket of the shirt.

There's gunpowder in the air. I can't smell it, but I know it's there because it leaves a sting.

Mary says, "It's a trick, isn't it? A trick gun."

"No," says Habril. "It's not a trick, Mary. It's a miracle. Akim is a gift of God. *Antab batak*. God's gift for the cause of Rapat. Akim Watabi, he whom God has chosen."

"Put the gun away, Habril," says Akim.

"In time," says Habril and levels the gun at Mary.

"For God's sake, put the gun away!"

I'm out of Habril then. Mary may not be trembling, but I am. With anger. As I exit, I feel the push of someone entering. Padua.

"How dare he!" I shout.

"Habril?" she asks, a little protectively.

"Yes, of course, Habril. He's a bully, a small-time bully. No, a big-time bully, he thinks he can . . . can just make things the way he wants by force. Because he's got a gun. Because he's got a bomb."

"Maybe," Padua says, "maybe when he doesn't use a bomb, or a gun, when he talks very softly, maybe no one listens."

"Oh, right, great." I am not speaking to Padua. I refuse. I brush right past her and float out to where I can get a decent view of Mary's face. She looks calm, serene almost. Maybe because she's gone to a point past feeling, maybe because, while I've been shrieking, Habril has actually put the gun away.

"Everything will go well for you," Habril says softly, bending to touch Mary under the chin, "just so long as Akim here completes God's mission." He looks up at Akim. "And Akim's going to do just that. It will be the first mission of many. In time, there will be nowhere in the world where Akim's face is not known, feared, loved." He pats his jacket pocket. "Am I right, Akim?"

Akim says nothing.

Habril straightens up. "Akim will also do it for you, Mary,

for his soulless little Christian friend. To keep you safe. But more than this, much more, Akim's going to act in memory of a woman who lived by the Southern Gate at Sacrini, a woman who laid her life on the line for him a long time ago, Mary. When Akim was a child and I—I was a youth called Omaz Lamyar. What were you called then, Akim? No—don't say anything. It doesn't matter. What matters is the woman. You remember the woman, Akim?"

"She didn't die of bullets," says Akim.

"No," says Habril. "But she did die. And do you know who she was? Do you even remember her name?"

"Lamyar," says Akim slowly, "Mrs. Padua Lamyar."

"Yes," says Habril. "My mother."

Akim opens his mouth to say something, and I'd open my mouth if I had one, in fact it would just drop open. Padua—Habril's mom! And I'm hovering there, feeling simultaneously amazed and shocked and angry, yes, angry, though of course it does explain her ludicrous affection for the man, when I begin to jig about. At least I think it's me jigging about, but then I realize it's Padua again. She's followed me out.

"Well, thanks for keeping me in the picture!" I say.

"Sorry," she says meekly.

"Sorry. Sorry! You bring your son up to be some trigger-happy bigshot with a bomb and he trains Akim and boom boom, bye-bye, Cassina. And you don't even have the guts to tell me."

"I never trained him," she says, "never wanted any of this for him."

"Can't have done much to stop it!" I say. I don't get Padua. She spins my droplets. Half the time she's Mrs. Altruistic, saving some kid she doesn't even know and the other half . . . "Whoa," I say. "What about that day at the olive grove? Habril was the boy with the metal slingshot, wasn't he? The boy who lent his slingshot to Akim."

"Yes," says Padua. "Yes."

"So is that why you did it? Helped the little boy? Some outrush of motherly guilt?"

"Why do you always need reasons for things, Cassina?"

"Because I want to understand. Is that so weird? Because I want things to make sense, and they don't right now. Not least how you let him do it. Habril, how you let him grow up a bomber!"

Padua sighs. "Of course, when a boy goes bad, it's the mother's fault. It's always the mother's fault, they say. And of course I've thought and thought about it. Thought of little else all these years. Where did I go wrong with my little Omaz? Or was it that I died, and then he had no one to protect him? Because they came to him, then, the radicals, they took him aside, whispered in his ears, renamed him, told him things. Holy things, of course. And he was a holy man. Is a holy man, Cassina. I believe that as surely as I believe in Ingali, angel of God. In his heart Habril is a holy man."

"Oh, right."

And then she floats away. Just like that, as though she had explained everything, as though there was nothing more to say, she floats back toward Habril. Her beloved, slaughtering son.

Habril and Akim are still arguing, or maybe Akim is apologizing and Habril, for once, is listening.

"I never meant it to be," Akim is saying. "I didn't choose for it to happen. For your mother to die."

"No, but she died anyway."

"Then believe me when I say I'm sorry."

"After all these years?"

"Yes, Habril, after all these years. I was only five. What could I have done? But I'm sorry, sorry for all your pain."

Habril puts his finger to his lips. "Then we won't speak of it again," he says. "We will not mention my mother's name again. But actions will speak. You will speak to God with your actions, Akim." He smiles. "You see, I never understood that death till now. But now—now I see God's divine purpose, working through my mother, through you, Akim. It is the time of delivery, of fulfillment. I am filled with joy." He stands up. "Now I have a little business to attend to. The time for talk is past."

Like mother, like son, eh?

He leaves the room, and I listen, as does Akim, to the locking of the apartment doors.

There's a short intake of breath, as though the room is settling around Habril's absence, and then Akim turns to Mary. "I'm so sorry," he says.

She's gone back to standing like a post. And I wonder if this is how she's coped all these years, with her absent father and her mad aunt and her evangelical mother, maybe she's got used to shutting down, shutting off, refusing things. I remember how, when I couldn't stand my mother's pain any longer, I hid inside Bonnie's head. Mary hasn't got that option. Where can Mary go but deep inside herself?

"Forgive me," Akim says. "Forgive Habril. The gun, it was a trick. You were right. A silly trick. He shouldn't have done it." And that's the father in him, I suppose, the father of the dead desert girl, trying to make things better, as they do, parents. I go to his face and allow myself to be swept up into his fissure, thinking, *Mary deserves this, deserves Akim, someone to care.*

"What killed the mother," Mary asks, "Habril's mother? What killed her if it wasn't the bullets?"

"I don't know," says Akim. In his brain there is a sudden heaviness, the breathless feeling of a child crushed beneath the weight of an adult. "I'm not sure anyone ever knew,

Mary. But it was a long time ago. A long, long time ago."

Akim cannot take his eyes from Mary's face; he's scanning each part of it as though he would commit it to memory forever: her elfin chin; her wide, frightened eyes; her mousy hair with wisps around the ears; her little pearly teeth with the gap up top where she must have lost her first couple of baby teeth.

"I love my mother," says Mary.

"I know. And your mother will be fine. Nothing's going to happen to your mother."

"I haven't got a father," says Mary. "Well, I have, but he doesn't come much."

"It's all right, Mary."

But it's not all right because she will not go to him, or let him advance to her. They stand opposed to each other, unmoving.

"Please, Mary. You have to trust me."

Nothing.

Akim changes tack. "Are you hungry? Maybe I could get you something to eat."

No answer.

"Thirsty? Although I think it's only water. Or maybe milk. We might have milk."

No answer.

"We could look in the fridge together."

"I want to go home," says Mary.

"Yes," says Akim. "I do, too."

Now Mary registers something different: surprise, curiosity. "I thought this was your home," she says.

"So did I," says Akim. "But I'm not so sure now."

"Can we go then?"

"Look." Akim goes through to the kitchen and jangles the door. "He's locked us in."

And that's when Mary, who has followed him as far as the doorpost of the kitchen, finally bursts into tears. The sobs are sudden and violent and totally defeated. But I feel quite glad about those tears because sometimes you need to cry, don't you? I've found that out being a para-spirit, because I've had to look at stuff and look at it again, with all my own tears dried up.

"Mary," cries Akim and cannot help himself from going to her and putting his arms about her. She remains stiff but unresistant.

And then something happens in Akim's brain, which I'm not sure I can describe exactly; but it's as if everything up until this moment had been in monochrome and suddenly all his lobes explode into color. Or maybe it's not about color, but about emotion; as if those things he used to think about—his dreams and memories—were (no matter how disturbing) still separate from him, videos he could slot in and out of his mind, and now the machine and the videos have become one, and there is no escape, no button to turn off the massive, overloading feelings of rage and love and powerlessness and grief that rip between all sections of his brain. I cower in my fissure, but also experience an excitement for I realize that Akim has been shadowy to me, a man recollecting himself from frozen pieces of the past and now, for the first time, I feel him uniting, becoming whatever, whoever he is now—Akim Watabi.

And I want to greet him, to say I'm sorry about the man who dropped your family's passes in the dirt, I apologize for the soldier whose jittery nerves fired the shot that killed your daughter. I'm sorry it was you who happened to be out that day at Southern Gate olive groves. "I'm sorry, Akim."

But the moment passes. Akim's brain settles into a quieter mode, and his arms drop away from Mary. Mary's sobs are exhausted. Together they sit down on the hard sofa. Mary is still holding the angel.

"May I see?" asks Akim.

And now she holds out the doll, its net skirt crumpled from being held so tightly in her hands. In Akim's mind the angel grows, it spreads its wings, it becomes Ingali, smiter and enfolder.

"I know," says Akim, trying to shake his own angel away. "Why don't we find it a tree?"

"What?" says Mary.

"The angel," says Akim. "Your angel—it's for a tree, isn't it?" He's concentrating so hard on Mary, on her battered angel.

"A Christmas tree," says Mary. "It goes right at the top."

"Then we'll get it a tree, put it right at the top."

Mary looks around the room, her eyes take in the upright chair, the black television set, the stack of videos, the old newspaper, the bare floorboards. "There isn't a tree," she says.

"Then we'll make one," says Akim.

If she was older—if she was me—Mary would laugh. But Mary just opens her wide eyes wider still and looks at Akim expectantly. Innocence, perhaps—but also faith?

Akim gets up and hunts about, as though there was something for him to find if only he looked hard enough. After two circuits of the bare room, he alights upon the newspaper.

"Here," he says.

Mary tilts her head.

"Trust me," Akim says. He takes the front page, the one with the pictures of me and Aelfin and the other bomb dead, and lays it aside. I'm glad about that. The paper is a tabloid and he opens the remaining pages in the middle and lays the whole on the floor, then, starting from the left-hand corner, he rolls the paper into a large cone. From a drawer in the kitchen he finds some scissors and a roll of tape with which he secures the basic shape. Triumphantly he stands it on the floor. It keels over.

Now Mary does laugh, and, oh, what an unexpected, sweet, sweet sound it is.

"I've an idea," she says and she scampers over to his side and tries to tuck in some of the excess paper around the base. Akim uses his thumb and forefinger to make the folds sharper and—hey—the "tree" stands up.

"What do you think?" says Akim.

"It looks like a hat," says Mary.

And it does; it looks like a witch's hat made of newspaper with scantily clad and upside-down women on it.

Akim takes the hat and puts it on Mary's head.

"You're a magician," he says.

"Or a dunce," she replies.

"Never," he says.

She takes the hat off. And you know what? I feel jealous. I'd like to be able to get down on the floor with both of them. I'd like to play too.

"We could try branches," says Akim. Taking the scissors he cuts little strips of paper up the sides of the cone.

"Let me try." Mary begins snipping; a couple of the branches get snipped off.

"Never mind," says Akim. "We can cut the inner layers, too." He bends some of the underlying strips so the top branches stick out more.

"What do you think now?"

"It's like a shaggy hat," says Mary. "But I like it."

"So do I," says Akim. A small wave undulates across his brain: *happy*. And I suppose he deserves this, too: the childless father holding out a hand to the almost fatherless child.

"But it should be green," Mary says.

They search the kitchen drawers for felt-tips or colored pencils, but there are only a couple of broken pencils and some black pens.

"Doesn't matter," says Akim. "We can imagine."

"Okay," says Mary. "This tree is green."

"You're right," says Akim. "The tree is green."

"And it smells," says Mary.

"Smells?"

"Yes, of course, all Christmas trees smell. Not nasty. Nice," says Mary. "They smell of pine and . . . and forests. It's a lovely smell."

"Right," says Akim, who is a T'lanni and therefore cannot be expected to know how Christmas trees smell. But he plays the game and sniffs. "Beautiful," he says.

"I'm going to put the angel on." Mary plumps up the net skirt of the angel, pushes her blond hair behind her plastic ears, and rearranges her silver halo. Then she places the offering on top of the cone.

"Wonderful," says Akim.

"It's too big," says Mary. And it is. The angel's skirt comes about a third of the way down the tree.

"Maybe it's not the angel that's too big but the tree that's too small," says Akim. "Perhaps we should make a bigger tree?"

"What with?" asks Mary.

"Umm." Akim scans the room. "Perhaps we could put the tree on top of the television, that would make it bigger, or look bigger anyway."

"No," says Mary. "That would be ugly."

"Then we could just not mind," says Akim. "As this is our tree and we made it, it doesn't have to be as big as a normal tree. It just has to be big enough for us."

"But things should be the right size," says Mary.

"Should they?" asks Akim.

"Yes. Things should be right."

"I think I've lost track of right," says Akim.

Oh, me too, Akim.

"Ornaments," says Mary. "It should have ornaments." She looks around her. "I know." She takes the page of bomb dead. "These are pretty."

"Pretty?" says Akim.

"Pretty faces," says Mary. "We can cut them out and stick them on."

Mary chops around the dead; she cuts me out, she cuts Aelfin out, she cuts out a big fat man with a beard. Akim just watches.

"Get me some tape," Mary says. "Please."

Akim does as he is asked, cutting small strips of tape and sticking them to the hard arm of the sofa. Mary peels them off one by one and adds the bomb dead to the Christmas tree. She sticks me at the foot of the tree and Aelfin next to the rim of the angel's skirt. No change there then.

"I killed those people," says Akim.

"Don't be silly," says Mary.

"No," says Akim. "Your aunt Lou was right. I killed them. I did it."

Mary pauses. "You can't have done it," she says.

"Why not? Why can't I have done it?"

"Because you're not a baddie," says Mary simply.

Akim's brain fountains: *Know this, Akim Watabi, your God sees all your deeds, done and undone.*

The lock in the door turns, Habril has returned. He comes into the living room and stares at the cut paper cone with the angel on top.

"What's that?" he says.

"It's a Christmas tree," says Mary. "Mine and Akim's."

"A Christmas tree," repeats Habril. "A Christ–mass tree. Yours and Akim's?"

"Yes," says Akim. "Mine and Mary's."

"What have they done to you?" asks Habril.

"Who?" says Akim.

Habril snatches at the tree, knocks the angel to the floor, and stamps on her.

"You're horrid," says Mary. "I hate you. Hate you, hate you, hate you."

"Do you know what an angel is?" asks Habril. "An angel—the angel—is Ingali, who smote the desert with the Word of God. An angel—the angel—is God's truth, who makes manifest the word of God as light brings shape out of darkness. An angel is *not*"—he grinds his heel on the angel's face—"something to be bought in a store!"

"She's only a child, Habril."

"And you are a man," says Habril. "Or were a man once, Akim. Akim, my brother, look at me."

Akim looks Habril in the eye.

"God loves you, Akim Saralli Watabi. *Antab batak.* Return to us, you who are chosen. Take His responsibility, He who is the One, the Only."

"Cassina, Cassina!" Padua bursts into the fissure. "Cassina, I know what he's going to do!"

"Okay, okay!" I reel backward.

"Sorry," she says. "Only I thought you'd want to know. I thought you were dying to know."

"Not dying," I say grimly.

"It's the mall," says Padua, "the shopping mall. On Saturday. Two Saturdays before Christmas. It will be packed. Who knows how many they'll kill? And if Akim refuses then Habril will shoot Mary. And he will, I know Habril. He would do it."

There is noise in Akim's brain because he's tussling with Habril, they're shouting about angels and only gods, but I focus all my attention on Padua. There is something I have to understand, and it all comes down to one question:

"Why?" I say.

"Holy Rapat," she replies.

"What?"

"Jihad." You understand *Jihad*? Rapat is for T'lannis what Jihad is for Muslims."

"You mean the war of believers against the infidels, the unbelievers?"

"Yes," Padua says. "No. I mean it's not that simple. I grew up among Muslims, and Islam is a religion of peace. *Jihad*'s just an Arabic word meaning 'striving hard.' It's used in the Holy Koran to mean striving to attain nearness to God by struggling to overcome your bad desires."

"But also striving to defend Islam?"

"Yes. But only if Islam is being attacked. Only ever for self-defense."

"And how is attacking a shopping mall self-defense?"

"It's not Muslims who are attacking the mall," Padua says sharply.

"Right, sorry, I apologize. But Rapat, it's the same, right, you said it was the same as Jihad?"

"Roughly, yes. And yes in the way some people have chosen to take the word *Rapat* out of context, make it mean something it doesn't mean."

And I wonder then about Mrs. Laney, about whether she ever took verses of the Bible out of context, if she made leaving Mary alone with strangers all right because of what the Bible did—or didn't—say?

"Though I do think," Padua continues, "that T'lannis have an obligation to bring their religion to others."

"Great way of bringing it. Great ad, slaughtering a few people in a shopping mall. People will be flocking to become T'lannis."

"You don't understand."

"Too right."

"You think—"

"Who thinks?"

"The West," says Padua. "You think you are not aggressors, but your power is everywhere. You beam your culture and your ways into our cities via television, via the Internet. We need clean water and medicines, and you give us expensive Coca-Cola and drugs your companies have dumped."

"Spare us the lecture, Padua."

But Padua doesn't. "There are walls you can see, Cassina, and walls you can't. Do you imagine that when we sit in the sand in the East, we can't see over the wall into your gleaming lives?"

"I thought you didn't want our 'gleaming lives.' That's what Habril said anyway. He thinks we're all empty; our 'gleaming lives' are just a mirage."

"Do you blame us for looking, Cassina? For needing to know?"

"I'm not sure I'm blaming you for anything, am I? Except the bombing, maybe."

"And then there's Sacrini," says Padua.

"Just one city, one piece of land."

"And one symbol of three thousand years of T'lanni oppression."

"Well, sorry, Padua, but the way I look at it, it still doesn't give you the right to bomb, to kill."

"Who's 'you'? I'm a T'lanni, for thirty-eight years T'lanni blood flowed in my veins, T'lanni stories in my mind. But I never joined Haliki. I don't support the bombing. I never have and I never will."

"You support Habril!"

"Habril is my son."

"Terrific, so morals go out the window if it's family!"

"Cassina, you're young. You didn't live as long as I did. I

tell you this, if you don't stand in the soft shoes of those pushed down; if you don't look at the world through their eyes just once; if you don't try to imagine then—"

"Then what? Then it's all my fault?"

"Then you haven't done enough."

There's a silence and then Habril bangs a door. He must have left the living room and returned again because he is now carrying two things: in his right hand a copy of the Holy Scroll and in his left a large canvas belt with six sewn—but as yet empty—pockets.

Padua begins to twitch. "I have to go," she says.

Mary looks at the belt. "What is it?" she asks.

"A killing machine," says Akim.

"A Holy Martyr's belt," says Habril. "For Saturday. *Antab batak.*"

13

"I don't understand," says Mary.

"It's quite simple," says Habril. "If Akim returns without detonating the bomb, I shall kill you."

He's sitting on one of the upright chairs and he's staring straight at her. I wonder what he sees.

"But your gun doesn't work," says Mary.

"Wait there," says Habril, as if Mary had the option of going somewhere. She watches him go into the kitchen and open the fridge. He returns with the melon with the slice cut out and sets it, slice side down, on top of the television.

"Observe."

"Is this really necessary?" asks Akim.

"I think so," says Habril. The melon is a cantaloupe.

Cruel, synapses Akim's brain, and then there's a wave which says *tired.*

Habril moves some distance from the television, seems to enjoy taking out the gun once more, leveling it at the fruit.

He pauses, puts something over the nozzle of the gun which I realize a moment later is the silencer, then he pulls the trigger. There's the short whoomph sound, and then the melon explodes. Seeds and pieces of orange flesh spatter onto the wall behind the fireplace. On the television top some remaining mush and a ragged piece of yellowy rind wobble.

"My gun works," says Habril peaceably. "Believe me."

Mary doesn't cry but she doesn't speak, either. Maybe she's getting used to Habril Fazheen.

"So," says Habril, smiling at Akim, "it would be wise to think carefully, my brother." He picks up his keys. "I have something to attend to, but I will be back in good time." He locks the doors on his way out of the apartment.

This time Akim makes no move toward Mary. There's a flatness about him, an exhaustion. Mary goes to the television and looks inside the exploded melon. She scrapes a piece of melon flesh from the wall with her fingernail. It has landed on the exhortation: *Repel evil wheresoever you shall find it.*

She turns her attention to the crushed cone Christmas tree and the broken angel. The angel's plastic face has a crack right across it, and its halo has become detached. Scattered across the floor are the trampled faces of the bomb dead. Mary picks up the picture of the fat man with the beard and sticks it over the angel's face using a piece of melon flesh for glue. She replaces the halo. The face falls off. The halo falls off.

"I hate him," she says. "Habril. I really hate him."

"We should clear up," says Akim tonelessly. He goes into the kitchen and gets a dustpan and brush. He sweeps up pieces of newspaper and melon seeds, discards the exploded rind, takes a wet cloth and wipes the top of the television set, uses toilet paper to dry the damp melon flesh spots from the walls. Mary sits on the floor in silence, holding the broken angel.

"We should throw that away," says Akim at last.

"No," says Mary. "I want it. We could mend it."

"I think it's past mending," says Akim.

Mary sits in unyielding silence.

"Tell you what," says Akim. "Why don't we pretend? Like

we did with the Christmas tree? Throw the plastic angel away and make a new angel. You could be the angel. How about that, Mary? No plastic angel, but a real angel! Mary Laney, angel."

"Habril says there aren't any angels. Well, only his one. The Ingali one."

"Well, I think," says Akim, "differently." And looking out of Akim's eyes, I see he has given Mary wings.

"Am I going to die?" Mary asks then.

"No, of course not," Akim says quickly.

"So you'll do the bombing?" She lifts her eyes toward him, but they snag on the sofa where the bomb belt lies.

"No," says Akim.

"But you did the other bomb, the station one. You said so."

"Yes," says Akim. "I did that."

"So why wouldn't you bomb the mall?"

"Because I survived, Mary. Because I looked, because I saw."

"Saw what?"

I could tell you that, Mary. Little old me, Cassina Dixon. Forgotten in Fissure. I saw CD racks falling and glass imploding and bodies twisting. And blood. Did I mention the blood before? No, maybe I kept quiet about that. It gets me when I'm napping, when I want a little para-spirit rest. That's when the blood comes. Into my never-shut eyes.

"I saw a girl," says Akim. "Maybe ten, maybe eleven years old. I didn't know her name then. But she was in the paper. You cut out her face. Aelfin, Aelfin Dixon. She fell, Mary; she died and her body—it lay on the ground the same way I dream my daughter Esta's body lay many years ago, when they shot her, soldiers. When she didn't look dead, but she was dead. And when I went past her—Aelfin—I should have felt victorious. That's what they told me I'd feel: Slaughter the enemy, spill their blood. I was primed and hungry for it. But when I saw the girl, I didn't feel that at all. I just felt like a father, a father with empty arms."

Oh, great speech. Give the man a clap. I mean, he couldn't have worked that out in advance? Used his brain, his *imagination*, to guess what it might feel like to actually do it? No. Too much to ask. But maybe that's it, why the recruits keep coming. Because most of them die, because most of them never have to look at the damage, actually put their fingers in the blood.

"If you don't do it," Mary says solidly, "then he'll shoot me."

"No," says Akim. "No! We'll make a plan. We'll do some more pretending. We'll say . . . say I've changed my mind, say I will go to the mall, that I will detonate the bomb. But only if he swears to let you go. I'll persuade him to let me take you to the mall. We'll have a sign. We'll tell Habril you need five minutes. You'll have to run, Mary, run like crazy, get out of the building. I'll give you time. When you're away you can stop an adult, find a policeman, tell him your address. You do know your address, don't you, Mary? You can go home."

"He'll find me," says Mary. "If you don't do the bomb, Habril'll find me. He'll shoot me. He will."

"No," says Akim. *Yes* flashes his brain and there's a sudden fireworking picture of a hundred bodies, a hundred dead strangers, but Mary alive, Mary smiling. And I'm sorry, I mean I've become really fond of Mary, but actually, wouldn't it be better for Habril to shoot just one child rather than for Akim to blow up who knows how many strangers? Strangers who also have families and lives. People like, for instance, me?

"What happens when you die, Akim?"

"You're not going to die, Mary."

"Mommy says you go to heaven."

"Yes, yes, of course you'd go to heaven, a child like you, of course." But in his brain there's a violent synapse: Jai'ur! *Mary's a* jai'ur, *an unbeliever, Mary cannot go to heaven. Mary will be left outside the gates, unable to gain access, forever abandoned to the outer darkness.*

"But Daddy said, Daddy said there's no such thing as heaven and hell. Daddy said heaven and hell are just made-up places, to keep you good, to make you afraid."

"Heaven . . .," begins Akim.

But Mary isn't listening, words are pouring out of her. "And Daddy said Jesus isn't the Lord of us all and Prince of goodness. Daddy said he didn't give a fig about Jesus because Jesus is the reason why he left us. Because Mommy liked Jesus more than she liked him. Because she kept bringing people into the house for Jesus. And if it wasn't for Jesus, we'd still be a happy family."

Jai'ur. Jai'ur! "Mary," says Akim urgently, "this is really important: do you believe? Do you believe in God, Mary?"

"Have you got a gun?" says Mary fearfully.

"No, no, it's not about that, Mary. I just have to know— what goes on in your heart." *Maybe*, his brain synapses, *maybe if she believes herself, in her Jesus, she can go to her own heaven. Mary will be all right.* And I think: too right, why can't you leave the poor child to the mercy of her own God? And then I think, uh-uh, why does Mary need to be all right anyway? She doesn't, unless you believe Habril will find her or else you do intend to detonate that bomb; And it creeps back into me then that Akim is a murderer, he has done it before.

"I don't know," says Mary. "I don't think so. I think I want my daddy. I do love my daddy, too."

"Mary," he says then, "about the sign; you know I said

when we go to the mall, I'll give you a sign, when you have to run?"

Mary nods.

"*Anatarah istali batak.*"

"What?"

"Say it, Mary."

"What does it mean?"

"I believe in the One, the Only God."

"I don't know. . . ."

"Say it, Mary!" And he's starting it, he's becoming like Habril, he's bullying her. "*Anatarah istali batak.*" I don't like this, I don't like it at all.

"*Anarah* . . ."

"*Ana*tarah, at, Mary, at."

"*Antarah* . . . I don't know. I can't do it."

"You can, you must." He takes both her hands in his and holds her tight. "And you must believe, you must believe it when you say it. *Anatarah istali batak.*"

"*Anatarah istali batah.*"

"*Bat*ak. *Anatarah istali bat*ak."

"*Anatarah istali batak,*" says Mary.

"Yes," says Akim. "Yes. Praise the Lord. Now one more time: *Anatarah istali batak*, I believe in the One, the Only God. Say it, Mary."

Mary says it—faultlessly.

"Good," says Akim, and he wipes his brow.

I have lost track of days, of weeks, of time, but it seems it's Friday.

"Tomorrow," Habril says, returning late, "is Saturday. Have you made your decision, Akim Watabi?"

"Yes," says Akim.

"And is it God's decision?"

"It is," says Akim.

"*Antab batak,*" says Habril. "God is just."

He goes to Akim and puts his arms around him, embraces him. Then he takes Akim's hands in his own and lifts them to his lips. "I have prayed for this moment." He reverently kisses the tips of Akim's fingers. "We will pray together now. We will spend the night praying."

"Mary must sleep," says Akim.

"Of course," says Habril, drawing away. "We'll make her a bed on the floor."

"She can have my bed," says Akim. "I will have no need of it tonight."

"As you wish," says Habril. "Well, Mary . . ." He looks around the room, as though he hasn't an idea where she is, finds her, sitting cross-legged on the floor. "Sleep well. Tomorrow is an important day. You and I, we will be here together, awaiting Akim's triumph."

"No," says Akim quickly. "Mary needs to come with me, don't you, Mary? To the mall. Or how will you honor your promise, Habril? You can't let her go from here. People might see, people might talk. Let her come to the mall with me and then, just before I . . . I do the Holy Act, I'll give her a signal, a kiss, and let her go. Let her get out. If they find her, they'll think she was confused by the bomb; if she says anything, anything about us, they won't believe her."

Habril swings his head from Akim to Mary, Mary to Akim. Mary is wise enough to keep quiet.

"You do intend to let her go," Akim says. "That is your promise."

"That is my word," says Habril. "My honor."

"Then let her come with me. It will be best. You'll see."

"As you say," Habril says at length. "But be warned, there is no hiding from Habril Fazheen."

"*Salanika*," Akim says, "*salanika*, my brother," and he gives a little bow.

Habril responds with a curt nod of the head.

"Come now," Akim says to Mary. "It's time to sleep." He holds out his hand.

Mary stands up. "I don't have any pajamas," she says.

"It's not cold," says Habril.

"Or a toothbrush."

"Come, Mary," says Akim and leads her away. In his bedroom he says: "Just take off your outer clothes. Keep on your shirt and, and . . ." He doesn't seem to be able to say the word *pants*.

She does as instructed.

"Now get into bed."

"I have to wash," says Mary. "Mommy says you have to wash before you go to bed."

"Yes, of course," says Akim. "Sorry. You know where the bathroom is."

In her absence he folds her clothes. When he hears the tap running, his brain synapses: *I offer you, my God, the sand of my heart on which to write your will.* And then there's a flash *tomorrow*, but no images come with the word, there is only whiteness, vacancy.

Mary returns. She looks pink-cheeked, and there's undried water around her mouth.

"I used my finger," she says, "for my teeth."

"Good," says Akim, and he folds back the sheet. "Get in."

"I have to do my prayers," says Mary.

"You said you didn't believe."

"But I say my prayers," says Mary. "I always say my prayers."

She kneels by the bed: "Our father, who art in heaven, hallowed be thy name, thy kingdom come, thy will be done, on Earth as it is in heaven. Give us this day our daily bread. And forgive us our trespasses as we forgive those who trespass against us. And lead us not into temptation. But deliver us from evil. For thine is the kingdom, the power and the glory, forever and ever. Amen." And then she adds, "And thank you, God, for today even though it hasn't been very nice. And God bless Mommy and Aunt Lou," and then lowering her voice to a whisper, "and Daddy." She pauses. "And God bless Akim. And also me. Amen."

Poor jai'ur child, flashes Akim.

Mary gets up and then reluctantly drops back down to her knees again, sighs.

"And God bless Habril," continues Mary. "And please forgive him about the angel and the Christmas tree. I'm sure he didn't mean it. Though I don't like him. Sorry about that, God."

She stands up again and gets into bed.

Akim's brain synapses *kiss,* and as he tucks her in, his body is drawn down to hers but he pulls back, leaves her be.

"Good night, Mary," he says.

"Can you leave the door open?" she asks.

"Yes," he says. "Of course."

"Akim?"

"Yes?"

"Will I be going home tomorrow?"

"Yes," Akim says. This time there's the crump of an explosion in his brain. "Yes."

Back in the living room, Habril has laid out a red mat, a jug of water, and two glass bowls. The scroll of the Holy Desert Words is open on the mat.

"Salanika," says Habril, and he kneels down to pour water into both bowls.

"Salanika," responds Akim and also kneels. Both men

wash their faces with their hands. There then begins a series of what seems like ritual pronouncements, with each man pausing between them to pour water on his forehead, his closed lips, the crown of his head, his rings. None of the water is wiped away; and by the end of the sequence both men are drenched, their heads, faces, hands, their upper bodies.

"You are a living martyr," says Habril.

"I am a living martyr," responds Akim.

"This is your free choice."

"This is my free choice."

"I call upon God to forgive your sins and bless your mission."

"*Antab batak.*"

"The power of the spirit pulls us upward."

"The power of material things pulls us downward."

"I make an oath on the Holy Desert Words." Akim puts his dripping face to the floor, touches the scroll. "*Hakamdaba, Lord. Fehadi mi'il. Anatarah istali batak.*"

"He makes the oath, the Rapat pledge. Let none come between him and his God now!"

Deep in the fissure I wait for Akim's brain to betray him. To whisper his real intentions to me. But Akim's brain is clear of everything but the prayers now, he is concentrating on each line, giving himself to the words.

"Battles for T'lanni freedom are not won through the gun but by striking fear into the enemy's heart," says Akim.

"And J'lal said, 'Ingali, bring me the souls of the martyrs, for them I love, they shall be with me in paradise forever.'"

"We will enter Paradise."

"Tomorrow will be the day."

"*Antab batak.*"

"*Anatarah istali batak.*"

Both men sit up on their heels.

"I am full of hope for you, my brother," says Habril.

"I, too, am full of hope," responds Akim. "Brother in God, brother in blood."

The men smile at each other. There are colors in Akim's brain I haven't seen before: violet-brown, the colors of Habril's brain, of his content. I realize I am used to Akim the man with a hole at the center of his life, Akim who is missing Esta and Manina, Akim who has space for Mary; but the violet-brown man is full up, full to overflowing. And I want to believe it's just the effect of the prayers, how they calm the men. But actually I don't think it is that in Akim's case. I think it's the *salanika* effect again, it's the feel of that word *brother*, because it still has a power, it seems to change things for Akim. It's as if, no matter how Akim distrusts Habril, hates him even, he still needs him. He responds to the brother who took him in when he had nowhere else to turn. And I want to say, "Hang on, Akim. Don't think about the brotherhood, don't get caught up in that all over again. Remember your great speech. Remember what you saw at the station, think of those other brothers and sisters! Remember you've changed. You said you'd changed!" But, of course, I can do nothing but sit inside Akim's brain and witness the warm violet-brown.

"Remember," Habril says, "the outcome lies in God's hands. He will decide. Who lives, who dies. We will see His will."

"The outcome," Akim repeats, "lies in God's hands."

That's when Mary screams. The pitch of the wail must cut through both men's brains because even Habril lifts his head.

Daughter. Akim's brain synapses through the mellow color and he pulls himself upright, pours himself through into the bedroom. Mary is barely awake, thrashing on the bed.

"Mary," Akim calls, "Mary." She fights and claws at him, wakes in her terror.

"What is it?" he cries.

"The dream!" Mary screams. "The dream!"

"What dream, what, Mary?"

Mary takes in the unfamiliar room, the unfamiliar man sitting on her bed, sobs.

"Tell me, Mary."

But Mary can't.

"Take a breath, Mary. Breathe in. Take a deep breath."

Mary takes a long hiccupy breath, stills. "It's the dream I always have," she says. "I'm standing on a cliff, and I know I'm going to fall. And my father's close by, so close I can reach out my hand and touch him. And I do reach out. But he doesn't take my hand. He looks, but he doesn't do anything. He lets me fall. At least I think he lets me fall. I don't know for sure. But that's when I always wake up. Just before I fall."

Akim says, "Mary, may I hold you?"

Mary bites her lip, nods.

So Akim holds her, holds her close. "I won't let you fall, Mary." But his brain is violet-brown.

In the doorway, Habril, who must have come to see what is taking so long, laughs.

14

All through the night the men continue to pray. Akim's brain becomes increasingly quiet, almost eerily so; it reminds me of how he was just after he was attacked in the park, when I thought he'd gone into some sort of hibernation. Only now the sense of peace is somehow more active, as if Akim has made a decision and is reconciled to it, so there is no need for any fizz-cracking because there is nothing more to be said.

Just after dawn there is a soft ring on the doorbell. Habril goes through to the kitchen, and I hear the sound of another man's voice, though I cannot distinguish what he is saying. The discussion continues in low tones for some minutes and then I hear Habril say, "Thank you, thank you indeed, my brother, may God go with you." I hear the outside door being opened again, shut, locked.

"Akim," calls Habril. "Come. Look."

Akim goes through to the kitchen. On the table is the suicide belt, only now its canvas pockets are full, bursting even, packed with explosives. I can see some sort of copper casing and wires, of course. But the whole thing looks dangerously DIY, like a bunch of fireworks strung together with a bit of telephone wire.

"It's not the same," says Akim.

"Yes," says Habril proudly. "A new design. This time we

have nitroglycerine. Thirteen pounds. We got fifteen but it wouldn't all fit. And also ball bearings. Our brother says they are more deadly than nuts."

Beneath one of the explosive packets is a bright orange switch. Akim's brain is calm, so calm. "And the detonator?" he asks.

"From a household drill. The switch of a Black and Decker. Only the best." Habril laughs. "Very sensitive, I understand." I wonder then whether Padua is laughing.

There's a noise in the living room, both men start and Habril instinctively covers the bomb belt with his arm. But it's only Mary, stumbling into the room still half asleep and turning on the television.

Habril looks at his watch. It's six o'clock.

"Kidnap victim linked to terror suspects," blares the early-morning news. A picture flashes up on the screen.

"That's me!" says Mary, becoming alert. It's a school photograph with Mary in a green-striped dress. I think how scrubbed she looks, how combed, how beaming.

"*Fal'kakka!*" exclaims Habril.

"Only before I lost my teeth," says Mary; and then she adds: "What does *fal'kakka* mean?"

"Martha Laney, the girl's mother, was too distressed to speak last night," continues the newscaster briskly, "but her aunt, Louise Bertish, made this statement. . . ." The picture dissolves to Aunt Lou, complete with face powder and extra lipstick and a large white bandage on her right temple.

"We are all devastated," announces Aunt Lou. She doesn't say the words *ax-murderer* but her eyes blaze them. "Who could do such a thing? Kidnap a child, hit an old lady?" She points at her temple. "Who could do it?"

"I want to go home," says Mary.

"*Fal'lamina ta'hili,*" says Habril. "This changes everything."

Aunt Lou disappears, and the newscaster moves seamlessly on to the exchange rates.

"She can't go with you to the mall," Habril says to Akim. "A T'lanni and a small girl. It would be too dangerous. They'll be looking for her everywhere."

Mary comes to the door of the kitchen. "I want to go home," she repeats. She sees the belt, curiosity draws her farther, she stretches out a hand.

"Don't touch!" screams Habril.

Mary stares at him, then pads back into the living room where she curls up on the sofa and changes TV channels. It's the cartoons. I hope they're really good this morning, I hope they last forever.

"Disguise," says Akim quickly. "You do it all the time, Habril. Why not disguise Mary? A hat, a scarf, a big coat—who would know?"

"No. It's too much of a risk."

"Not as much of a risk as letting her go from here either."

"She needn't go from here," says Habril. "I could drive her. Drop her miles away."

"A haircut," says Akim. "Boys' clothes maybe . . ."

"No." Habril goes through to the living room, grabs the television remote, and snaps off the cartoons.

"Why d'you do that?" says Mary. "Why do you spoil everything?"

"This is a big day, Mary. Haven't you got anything better to fill your head with?"

"I know it's a big day," she says. "I'm going home."

Home. Oh, Mary.

"Please?" says Akim. "I promised Mary I wouldn't let her fall. You heard me promise, give my word. Do you want her to think T'lannis are not men of honor? That we don't honor our word?"

"It's not to do with that," says Habril.

"You promised," says Mary, staring straight up at him. "You said I could go to the mall with Akim."

"Things have changed," says Habril.

"Honor doesn't change," says Akim.

At nine a.m. Habril leaves the apartment, returning within twenty-five minutes with some boys' jeans, a boys' leatherette flying jacket, and some black hair dye—permanent.

"What's that for?" asks Mary.

"Go in the bathroom," instructs Habril.

"Why?"

"Go," says Akim, "please, Mary."

Mary goes. Habril opens the hair-dye box and takes out a gunmetal gray tube of hair tint and squeezy bottle of Crème Developer. There's also an instruction leaflet stuck to the back of which is a pair of see-through plastic gloves. Habril peels them off.

"What are you going to do?" asks Mary.

"It's only hair dye," says Akim. "To stop people recognizing you. To make you safe when you come with me."

Habril puts on the gloves. It reminds me of the gloves the embalmer wore when she pumped formaldehyde into my sister's dead body.

Habril pierces the opening of the color tube with the spike in its own top and then squeezes slugs of pale brown tint into the developing bottle.

"I thought it was supposed to be black," he says.

"It will go black, I'm sure," says Akim.

But it doesn't. Even when he shakes it, the lotion remains a dirty beige only now streaked with gray.

"We need a towel," says Akim.

"What for?"

"To put around her shoulders. Cover her clothes. In case we spill any."

"She won't need those clothes again," says Habril. "Put your head over the basin, Mary."

"No," says Mary.

"If you don't, I'll force you," says Habril.

Mary puts her head over the basin.

"How are you supposed to apply it?" asks Habril.

"Here—let me," says Akim. He takes the gloves from Habril and I prefer them on his hands. He rolls up his shirt-sleeves and then he points the nozzle of the bottle into the depths of Mary's hair.

"'Work through thoroughly from root to tips,'" reads Habril.

Akim massages the lotion into Mary's hair.

"It smells disgusting," says Mary.

"'Leave for twenty minutes,'" reads Habril.

Bubbly spots of the mixture go on Akim's arms and on the basin. Where he wipes the color from his flesh, it leaves an inky blue stain. There are also dark wet stains on Mary's red top.

"Put your head back, Mary."

Mary stands up straight, flips her hair back. I see—and so do the men—the blue stains along the line of her forehead and on the top of her ears, the streams of blue down her cheeks.

"Idiot," says Habril and attacks her face with soap and water.

"It's getting in my eyes!" Mary cries out.

"It'll come off with the rinsing," says Akim. "We have to rinse her hair."

"It's not twenty minutes yet," says Habril. "We need to get it off. It has to come off. She looks ridiculous. We need a nailbrush."

"We don't have a nailbrush."

Habril grabs a toothbrush and starts a vigorous scraping of Mary's forehead.

"Ow. Ow ow ow." And do you know what? There's not a single fizz-crack in Akim's head. No, "Come on, Habril, that's enough." Or, "Be a bit more patient." Or simply, "For goodness' sake!" And I'd like to think it's because Akim knows how important it is for Mary to look the part, how Habril won't let her go to the mall if she's instantly recognizable as Mary Laney, kidnap victim, but I'm not sure anymore. I don't like the quiet. Padua said he went quiet when he tried to forget things, forget Manina, forget Esta. What exactly is Akim trying to forget now?

Mary begins to cry. Her hairline is blue where the dye has not come off and red where Habril's been scraping. But he still scrapes until Akim says it's time to rinse.

Mary puts her head back over the basin and Akim turns on the taps. Blackish water pours off her hair. Akim rinses and rinses until the water runs clear. The basin is streaked gray, so Akim rinses that, too.

Meanwhile Habril towels dry Mary's hair, pulls her in front of the mirror.

"What do you think?"

Her hair is jet black, blue-black, like Superman's in the comics. It is completely the wrong tone for her flesh, which, where not scraped red, is sallow. She looks like a magazine picture I once saw of a Chinese child with tuberculosis. She also looks totally miserable.

"It's not me," she says in a small, sobby voice. "I'm not me anymore!"

"Good," says Habril. "Success."

Next they dress her. She's gone very, very quiet now, her white-post mode. She doesn't protest at all as Habril pulls on the jeans (slightly too big) and wraps the flying jacket (absurd on a child as slim as Mary) about her. But, of course, it is a success because I'm not sure even Martha Laney would recognize her daughter now.

But Habril is still not satisfied. He goes into the kitchen and returns with a large pair of scissors.

"No," says Mary without conviction.

Habril chops anyway. Large handfuls of black hair fall on her shoulders, on the floor. He brushes hair from the fake sheepskin of her jacket collar. Gradually she changes from ill Chinese child to street-urchin Goth. She makes no remark about her changing appearance, just stands in a kind of stupefied silence as though her brain has overloaded and temporarily shut down. It makes me want to go into her brain and rewire her, make her smile again.

"You, too, must change," says Habril to Akim when he's finished with Mary. "Shave your head."

"If you believe so."

"It's necessary." Akim kneels on the bathroom floor and Habril sets about him with the scissors. Mary drifts away, back into the living room though there is little enough to do there. When Akim's head is shorn, Habril takes a razor to finish the job. He soaps Akim's head and shaves him to the scalp. He makes one small nick, and a bead of blood appears which he wipes away with the back of his hand. Akim says nothing. When Habril has finished, Akim looks at himself in the mirror. He looks smaller than he did before and more vulnerable. I can see a vein in his head where the blood pulses.

Padua comes then.

"Habril's going to go, too," she announces. "To the mall. He doesn't trust Akim, he's decided to go, too."

Pushed into the depths of the fissure, I say, "Don't you do sorry or excuse me or good morning anymore?"

"Good morning," says Padua.

I regroup. "So he can't be expecting Akim to detonate the bomb, then. Otherwise he'd get blown to smithereens, too."

"No, he's got telescopic sights. That's where he went the other day. To get a gun with telescopic sights. So he'll be able to see Akim, only keep his distance, just in case."

"A guy looking through a gun with telescopic sights? In a shopping mall? I don't think everyone will be that interested in their Christmas shopping. I think they'll notice, Padua."

"No they won't because he's also got binoculars, tiny ones. Smaller than opera glasses. He'll use them to start with and only bring out the gun if necessary. Will it be necessary, Cassina?"

"How should I know?"

"Because you've been here. Because Akim must have said."

"Wrong," I say. "He's been as silent as the grave. Excuse the pun. Listen yourself."

We are both silent. Not a single zap passes the surface of Akim's brain.

"See?"

"He's afraid," says Padua quietly.

"How do you work that out?" I ask.

"Afraid," repeats Padua.

"But not as afraid as I am, that's for sure." I pause. "What's it like, Padua, being blown up as a para-spirit? I mean, you've been through it, at the station."

She exhales a sort of soft, wet sigh. "Loud," she says finally. "Deafening. I didn't stop reverberating for about twenty-four hours."

"Terrific. But it doesn't hurt hurt?"

"And I didn't like the blood," she adds.

"We don't have any blood. Do we?"

"No," she says. "But the humans do."

"Right. Well, I'm with you there. I don't go for the blood much, either."

I shut up then. I'm not sure I want to hear any more.

"I'll swap," Padua says. "I'll go with Akim, if you want."

"Why would you want to do that?"

"Just an offer," she says. "Your choice."

And there it is again. The contradiction that is Padua, Mrs. Motherly, Mrs. If-Anyone-Should-Get-Hurt-It-Should-Be-Me, and Ms. Better-Be-at-the-Center-of-the-Action, as she was at the Southern Gate, as she was when she accompanied Akim on his first bombing raid. Which makes me realize that I want to be in the center of the action, too. I feel I owe it to Akim, to Mary, and also to myself. So that even if my father knocked on the door right now, and I could hitch a ride home in his brain, I don't think I would. I think I would have to go to the mall. And it's not just suicidal curiosity, it's that I don't think I've quite given up the idea that I can make a difference, intervene.

"No," I say. "Thanks."

"Suit yourself."

Then something occurs to me about the gun. "If he shoots Mary," I say, "then the game's over anyway. Akim will never detonate the bomb then."

"The gun's not for Mary," says Padua. "The gun's for the bomb."

"What?"

"Akim can press the drill switch. Or Habril can just fire a bullet straight into the nitroglycerine."

And, of course, I hadn't thought of that. I'd just thought of Mary running and, when she was safely away, maybe Akim running, too. Getting away from Habril. But, of course, there is no getting away from Habril.

"Do you still want to go?" Padua asks.

"Yes. If I don't come back . . ."

"You will come back," Padua says.

"Are we friends?" I try then.

"We're not enemies," says Padua.

What did I want her to say? Good luck?

"Good luck," she says, "Cassina."

And I return, "Good-bye."

"Nothing's ever quite good-bye," she says, and then she's gone.

The men are beginning to dress. For himself Habril has chosen black chinos, a dark shirt, and a casual, nondescript navy jacket with a hood. For Akim he has laid out a pair of brown corduroy trousers, a long-sleeved white shirt, a loose-fitting black woolen overcoat, and a pair of black socks, and black slip-on shoes. Akim puts on the trousers and the socks and shoes, and then follows Habril, bare-chested, into the kitchen.

"It is the time," says Habril.

"The time," repeats Akim. *"Antab batak."*

He turns his back to Habril and, very gingerly, Habril lifts the bomb belt from the table. He passes it around Akim's waist. There's no buckle, just a couple of ties made of material the width and color of bandages. Habril draws the belt tight, pulls the material gently into a knot. Akim moves one of the wires where it presses into his stomach.

"Does it feel secure?" asks Habril.

"Yes, God willing," says Akim. He puts on the white shirt, wearing it loosely, not tucked in. I see his hand go underneath.

"And the detonator?" queries Habril.

"By my right hand," says Akim.

"The right hand of God," says Habril.

"Salanika," they say together.

Salanika.

"Then we are ready," says Habril. "Come."

Akim puts on the coat.

"Mary," he calls softly.

A tousled, black-haired boy arrives.

"Mark," says Habril. "Your name is now Mark."

"Yes," says Mary.

"In the car there will be total silence, Mark. You understand?"

"Yes," says Mary.

Akim takes her hand, gives it a squeeze, but it is to Habril
that he turns. *"Salanika,"* he says. "My brother."

15

Habril parks a few minutes' walk from the shopping mall. I know exactly where we are because this is the road where my mother used to park when she brought Aelfin and me to buy school shoes or stationery, or get us clothes or drop me to meet a friend. For this is my mall that Akim intends to blow up, my local hangout. It has four levels: an underground garage ("outrageously priced" according to my mother, which is why we always had to park in the street); two levels of shops; and then, at the top, a floor devoted to cafés and fast-food outlets. My friend Sophie and I used to go regularly to Starbucks, stir one whipped-cream caffe mocha between us and talk about the big stuff: sisters (Sophie had an annoying one, too), parents, boys, nail polish, Robbie Williams. Sometimes we'd also go to Bon Bons and have a chocolate-flavored magnificent ice and two spoons. Though they threw you out faster in Bon Bons.

Call me sentimental, or call me simply frightened, but I don't feel too good sitting in the car and looking at my mall this morning. I observe the structure of the place, the attractive blue flying buttresses which make the outside of it look like a cross between a cathedral and a circus tent. The buttresses are made of steel, I know they are, but somehow, they look flimsy. The entrance is huge, inviting, and made entirely of glass. I never noticed this before—how much glass there is in this mall.

"And J'lal said: 'Ingali, bring me the souls of the martyrs, for them I love, they shall be with me in Paradise forever,'" says Habril.

Akim gets out of the car, Mary gets out of the car. Habril remains where he is. "God go with you, *antab batak*."

"*Antab batak*," repeats Akim. "Come, Mark."

Mary walks in Akim's shadow and neither of them turn to look back at the car, so neither of them know whether Habril stays or drives away. So I don't know, either. I want to float out of Akim's head to check, see what Habril's up to, find out if he's really going to follow us. But I remain where I am. Of course Habril will follow us, not because Padua said he would, but because that's the sort of man he is: precise, thorough.

Mary is not keeping up, she's lagging, her feet scuffing the pavement. Akim turns to wait for her, and when I see her face, I have a sudden vision of a china doll with a dark crack through her right eye and her porcelain white cheek. Or maybe it's that angel Habril stamped on.

"Are you afraid?" asks Akim.

"Yes," says Mary. It's barely a whisper.

"Don't be," says Akim.

"Mommy . . .," begins Mary.

"Have faith."

"Mommy," continues Mary with a kind of spill, "my mommy will cry. And Aunt Lou. And Bister will miss me. And Daddy. I think Daddy will miss me."

"Faith, child." In Akim's brain there's a flutter of something for Mary, not something big or expansive, just something very light, very gentle, which is followed by a quick synapse: *She cannot fall. This is my word. Mary must not fall.*

"Come," Akim says.

And despite everything, she comes, she follows him, obedient to the last.

They arrive at the doors of the mall which slide open for

them and the twenty other people who choose at that moment to move either into or out of the mall. And I think of those who are leaving and how, maybe later in the day, they will thank their gods or their stars for whatever it was that made them depart early, leave in time. How they'll rerun the decision in their minds, how they had to make lunch or get to Grandma's or buy a garden rake and how, maybe, that lunch or that visit or that rake saved their lives. I imagine how they'll clasp their loved ones and cry when they think of those others, the men and women and children coming into the mall alongside Akim and Mary and me right now, whose fate, perhaps, was different.

The mall is designed like a wheel with three spokes. In the very center of the wheel is an open atrium with a glass elevator that travels between all floors. You come into the mall (along any one of the three spokes) on the upper level and need to take the elevator or escalators down to the lower level and garage, or up to the restaurant level. On the lower level, in the central space by the elevator where they normally have car promotions or companies selling beanbag sofas, today they have Santa's Grotto. Santa himself is concealed from view, hidden inside some snow-topped grass mound, but the waiting line snakes around a lidless maze of animated figures, furry woodland creatures in little red blazers playing musical instruments and singing Christmas carols. On the glass balconies which overlook the atrium on each level, people crowd to point down at the snowy scenes of hedgehogs and moles and bushy-tailed squirrels. Animals, I think then, who should be hibernating.

Along each of the spokes of the wheel huge Christmas lights are hung, and miles of industrially rigged gold tinsel and twinkling fairy lights. We come along the spoke past a double-level bookshop, HMV, the Disney Store, two jewelers, Accessorize, the Gadget Shop, a very expensive designer sports shop, and Girl Heaven. I imagine, just for a moment, how it would be to be making this journey in Habril's brain: how much he would hate it, how much the ping of cash registers would offend him; buy, buy, buy even if you don't need, need, need. And what's there to need here? It's all flimflam, all glittering trash. No, no it's not actually, there are books here, there's music. And what about the need to allow oneself some frippery, something garish or silly or gay? A little pom-pom, a sparkly butterfly for your hair? What would Habril's world be, stripped of these things? Would it be loving and moral and good and full of people with high and beautiful thoughts, or would it be bleak and empty and lacking in laughter?

Nobody looks at Akim; nobody looks at the dark-haired "boy" beside him. They are too busy with their Christmas shopping after all. They are rushing and waiting in line and paying and laughing and barging and chatting and arguing and going about their business. They do not know how close they are to paradise.

Akim walks Mary to the central atrium, where the elevator is.

"You are going to do it," she says, "aren't you?"

"You'll be safe," said Akim. "I've said that. Promised it."

"I don't think God will like it."

"Tell me your address," says Akim.

"I wouldn't like it, if I was God," she continues, oblivious. "It would make me sad. It would make me cross. Like I made something beautiful, and someone else stamped on it."

"Your address," demands Akim. "Tell it to me again."

"Thirty-three Kilne Road."

"Good. And remember when I give you the signal, the kiss, go immediately. Don't run. Not at first. Just walk. Very fast, but walk. Then run. When you're on the street, don't look back. Say you're lost. Ask for help. Don't ask a man unless he's a policeman; ask a woman, a woman with children of her own. Understand?"

Mary looks around, below to the grotto where children in strollers are waiting in line with their mothers to meet Santa Claus, and up to the crowded glass balconies above, where the people stand and point. As she turns about I scan the mall for Habril. Down the second of the spokes, I see a man standing still, which is why I notice him because everyone else is moving and he's just standing there. He's not wearing a navy jacket, he's wearing a thick leather jacket and a black woolen ski cap, but of course Habril might have changed, would have changed, surely? It would have taken him no time at all. At the man's eye level, something glints. And of course it could just be a pair of ordinary glasses. But the man stands like Habril, is his height, his build, so I think it's the binoculars.

"Concentrate," says Akim.

Mary also looks down the second spoke. "If you don't do it, Habril will come for me, won't he?"

"You'll be safe. I give you my word. But you must concentrate, you must do everything that we've agreed." His brain synapses *jai'ur,* and it's a difficult, hard flash, but then he soothes himself again, and his next synapse is violet calm: *I believe in the destiny of my own deeds, that whatsoever I do well in this life will do well for me in the afterlife and whatsoever I do ill will go ill for me in the afterlife.* He takes a deep breath. *Soon,* his brain murmurs. *Act with care. Find the right place.* We are close to the elevator, he has a view along each spoke and down to the lower level and up to the restaurants. There's a girl leaning over the balcony by Starbucks. Two girls. I don't believe it, it's Sophie, Sophie with Serena Garth. How can Sophie be having coffee with Serena Garth! The also-ran, the girl who always hung around us, sat too close, wanting to be part of the group, only she wasn't, couldn't be, whining little Serena Garth! We laughed at her, Sophie and I, and now, and now! Well, it sure makes me feel dead. One hundred percent dead. If Sophie is having coffee with Serena Garth. Bye-bye, world. Why would I care?

But, Sophie—oh, my goodness, Sophie. Run, Sophie, get out, get out now. And Serena, you might as well run too; being blown up, it's not so great, your mom wouldn't want it for you. "Run!" I yell. Only of course I don't, and Sophie and Serena continue to lean over the edge of the balcony and smile.

"This way," says Akim. He steers Mary down the third spoke, toward Debenhams and Claire's Accessories and away from the atrium and the children waiting in line to see Santa Claus.

"What would you like for Christmas, Jamie?"

"A gun, Santa, a sword . . . a big red bomb."

Akim's right hand moves beneath his shirt, he's feeling for the explosive belt, for the orange switch that once belonged to an electric drill. I can hear his breath hard in his throat and all of a sudden he's sweating. His left hand goes to his collar, peels it away where it's sticking to his neck. He swings his head right and left and then looks over his shoulder, as if he knew he was being watched. But I can't see Habril now, there are too many people, all of them moving.

"When I give the word," Akim says to Mary, "go straight into Debenhams. We're on the street level. You need to go down a level, follow the garage signs. You can get out through the garage. That'll be safer. Just follow the exit signs. Understand?"

"Will I see you again?" asks Mary.

"Do you understand!" says Akim, raising his voice, so

people near turn to look. And the violet edges of his brain snap into deep, angry purple.

"Yes," says Mary, recoiling. "Yes, I think so."

"Good." He takes her hand.

"But where are you going? What are you going to do?"

"Don't worry about me," says Akim.

She turns her face up to his, white against the black of her hair. "But I like you," she says shyly. "I love you."

Then Akim's head fills with angels. Not the one angel, not Ingali with his powerful wings and his smiting hands, but a multitude of lesser beings, cherubs clothed in a white so bright they fill my fissure with blinding light. Each cherub has a different face, only as they turn and look out of Akim's memories and dreams they are also all Marys, all Estas. Their hair is the light brown that Mary's was before Habril pushed her head under Raven dye, their noses are Esta's baby snub, their eyes are wide and brown and they are all missing teeth, so the cherubs smile a million gap-toothed smiles.

"Mary," says Akim.

"Mark," says Mary.

Akim leans down as if he would kiss her, and, as fast as they have come, the cherubs disappear and in their place is a hard synapse: *Paradise is very, very near—right in front of our eyes. It lies beneath the thumb. On the other side of the detonator.* And that's when I realize Akim has not once taken his hand from the electric drill switch.

"Say it, Mary," whispers Akim, his lips not quite at her cheek. "Say it. *Anatarah istali batak.* I believe in God, the One, the Only."

And with the words comes a sudden, explosive noise, like the crashing of water over a huge precipice, only it isn't water, it's too rhythmic, too controlled; it's wings, it's the beat of a giant pair of wings. It's louder than the universe, and it's inside Akim's head.

And it comes to me then what Akim intends to do. What he means by not letting Mary "fall," because souls borne aloft by Ingali don't fall, do they? They never fall, they remain uplifted forever, in bliss forever, but only if they are not *jai'urs*, only if they believe in the one holy, only God. If they're martyrs. And I can't believe I've been so stupid, so slow. And I reckon I have less than a minute to act, but I cannot act, cannot do a thing because I'm a para-spirit.

"*Anatarah . . .,*" begins Mary.

"No, Mary," I cry. "Don't say it. The moment you've said it, he'll press the button!"

". . . *istali . . .,*" says Mary.

I'm out of Akim, putting the whole force of my negligible droplets against Mary's face. "No!"

". . . *batah,*" says Mary.

"*Batak,*" says Akim. "Again, Mary, again."

"*Anatarah . . .*"

Go into her brain. Of course. This is the answer, or at least the one thing I could do that might make a difference. Children's brains are only partially formed, that's what Blacoe said, so maybe they're more malleable; maybe if you speak inside a child's brain, they actually listen, they hear you. Minor point: it's against the rules; "first come first served on hosts and no going into children." But who makes up the rules? Blacoe never really did answer that one. Besides, what sort of damage could I do to Mary that would be worse than her being blown limb from limb? I mean even if I killed her—what difference is that going to make? Zero seconds to decide.

"Sorry, Mary, this is for your own good."

I beat a furious path up her nostrils and into her brain, making, by instinct, for the fissure. But there is no fissure. In fact there are no deep cracks or cavities or divisions in Mary's brain at all. There's just one pulsing, vulnerable joined-up whole, so delicate, so moist it could make a para-spirit weep with refreshment. Or it might if it wasn't for the dizzying pictures, at least I find them dizzying at first because they seem to overlap, like photographs taken on top of one another. An image of Mrs. Laney is superimposed on a picture of Bister the dog and Mary's father with his suitcase and behind this is a small sandy beach and a rock pool with a crab and in front of it a fairytale castle with blue turrets and silver flags which might be Sacrini but which can't be, and so the images continue like mirrors reflecting mirrors, as if all of Mary's life lay here, unsorted, waiting for her to decide what to prioritize, what to make important, who or what to love.

"Don't say the words!" I screech, which is a mistake, as Mary's head lurches wildly to the left and all the pictures smash and bang and jumble into each other.

". . . the one, the only Thirty-three Kilne Road," says Mary.

And I'm too late because she has said the words even if she's also added her address and I can see that Akim's still coming for the kiss. So maybe I'm wrong, maybe it's the kiss that seals her fate, or the words and the kiss together. And I remember the kiss and the death in the desert, and I haven't time to think through things logically so I just force my way back into the air, to put what little there is of me between his lips and her cheek. As I go I shout, "Duck, Mary!" and this time I mean to shout, to scream. And she does duck, or at least her head swerves again so that Akim's pursed lips land not on her cheek but on my concentrated droplets.

Then the world explodes. And I think Akim has pressed his thumb on the detonator and it's all over, another fiasco courtesy of Cassina Dixon, another crisis she spectacularly failed to avert. And then I realize that things are not so much exploding as imploding. Or maybe it's just me imploding, it's difficult to keep track of what's happening around me because of the boiling. Each one of my droplets is becoming hotter and denser and bigger. It's like I'm the Big Bang theory in miniature, I'm a kind of detonating cosmic egg, a mix of expanding matter and pure energy. And for a moment (or perhaps for an eternity—who can tell?) I feel quite good; elated, sparky (forget brain-zaps— I'm the Blackpool Lights on speed), and then the heaviness kicks in, as if each of my increasingly large droplets is being shaped, molded, squashed into some particular form and then covered in a thick layer of molten flesh. And I look down then and that's what it is—flesh. It's unreal, I'm about the size of an ordinary human now, about my own size in fact. Cassina Dixon, age 13, and right in front of my eyes (which means, I presume, I have a face?), I'm growing flesh. No, not growing it, accumulating it, it's covering what I thought was hardening droplets but what turns out to be expanding muscle and bone. In short, I am getting a body.

That body continues to take form, to become more detailed so that my arms gain hands and then fingers and then fingernails, and even, at the base of my thumb, a little mole I was born with. And that's what it feels like, being born, watching yourself into creation. It's exhilarating but over all too soon. I know when it's finished, when I'm complete, because the feeling of energy slides away, and I'm left with this great, lumpy inert thing. Me.

But you could still knock me down with a feather. Actually, you wouldn't even need the feather, I'd fall over anyway, nearly do fall over. Because it's so heavy this body; after being a para-spirit it's like being encased in concrete. I don't have any sense of balance, I lurch, I'm like some Mummy of the Dead, only I'm not dead. I'm alive. I can't believe it, I'm alive! If I could move one foot with any safety, I'd dance. I really would, even though I don't do dancing, didn't anyway. Before. As it is, I just concentrate on trying to stay upright and look about me, get my bearings.

There hasn't been an explosion, not one for the people in the mall anyway. They're all still there. Still here. Most of them continue to go about their business, shopping, chatting, barging. The noise of them comes to me like an ill-tuned radio, loud and distorted, as though my senses haven't quite come back to me yet. And I shake my head, as if there was water in my ears, and that also nearly makes me fall, but I hear something then, hear it very loud, though part of me knows it's a woman whispering.

"Disgusting," she says.

A small crowd has gathered near us, they come slowly into focus. They are staring, some of the children are pointing. Am I that unusual? I look down at myself. Yes, I am unusual for somebody in a shopping mall. I'm stark naked.

I lurch forward to the nearest stroller and grab a white baby blanket and cover myself up. The front half of me, anyway. Anyone behind me will have an uninterrupted view of my butt-end, but I can't think about that now because the radio is coming into clearer focus, and it's Mary's voice I hear.

"I hate you," she says. "Hate you, hate you, hate you. You've killed him."

I follow her gaze to the marbleized floor of the mall, where Akim lies on his back, totally still. And at first I think I must have knocked him down while I was busy exploding into being, or maybe when I was lolloping around like some overgrown dog, but then I hear his breathing, or rather his not breathing. Because with all the other noise, I realize I can hear the breath of every person in the mall, their soft ins and outs, the regular breaths and the irregular, the chokes, the wheezes, the sighs, the catches, but from Akim I can hear nothing. I drop to my knees, steady my dizziness, put an ear to his nose, his mouth. Nothing.

"He's dead," someone says. And it's me.

Then I hear two noises simultaneously, a bursting sob from Mary and, some hundred yards away, a whoomph followed by a fast, hissing sound. The hissing sound gets louder. I scan the balconies and there he is, Habril, and I know it's him not just because, alongside my hear-every-thing-extra-loud ears I seem also to have acquired see-everything-horribly-accurately eyes, but because of his still figure and the glint of what has to be a gun because I can also see the bullet. It's traveling toward our little group at astonishing speed. Only I see it in slow motion, not as the blur it must really be, but as a tiny, perfectly shaped golden missile with a rounded, deadly head.

To the astonished gasps of the onlookers, I punch Mary away, fling her to the ground. She lies some way from Akim, completely quiet, the crying stunned out of her. And I know what I must do, of course, because I know where the bullet's headed. It's perfectly on target for the suicide belt around Akim's waist. And it's only a matter of milliseconds before it will arrive and this is my moment, my Cassina Dixon Hero moment, the one I seem to have been wanting all my life, all my half-life, the moment where I make a difference, the point at which I become someone my mother is proud to own newspaper articles about: Cassina Dixon, Mall Heroine, the girl who, with no regard for her own safety, flung herself across the suicide bomber, absorbing the full impact of the bullet, and so preventing the detonation of the bomb and saving scores of lives.

Only one problem; to do this heroic thing, I, Cassina Dixon, have to take the bullet, have to die again. And I'm not sure that I can bear it. I mean I've only just arrived back and I quite want to see my mom and give her a little hug, and chat to my dad, and see if Sophie makes it, and take Bonnie out for a walk and . . .

And there's no time to think. And what's the point anyway because if I don't do it (the bullet is coming so very slowly) then I'll die anyway, along with everyone else. Besides I owe these bystanders their lives. Because I didn't save Aelfin. In fact, you could say I caused her death, led her to be in the wrong place at the wrong time, and so now it's payback time, my chance to redeem myself. I'm doing it for you, Aelfi. And also perhaps for Mary, who I think I've come to love, too. And also perhaps for decency, because it's the right thing to do. It *is* the right thing to do.

Isn't it?

I throw myself, clumpily, over Akim. I try not to fall too hard, of course, in case I detonate the fireworks myself, but physical coordination still seems largely outside my control. Still, there's no bang so I have to assume this part of the operation is a success. I deliberately lie my back to his stomach so I still have the little baby blanket to cover my decency. Or indecency. It's a small thing in the light of what's just about to happen, but there's no point offending people just for the sake of it. Anyway, I shut my eyes then. The bullet is still on its way, I can hear its endless whiny hiss. But I don't have to look at it, do I? Don't have to watch it enter my lovely new-made body. And I do love this body. I could have had fun with this body, admired it, cherished it, never complained about the size of its butt, my butt. We could have gone places together, my body and me. As it is, I lie here behind my eyelids, in a dark of my own making, determined to spend my last few nanoseconds being grateful for these few blessed moments of life, for the extraordinary experience of creation. Not everyone gets to see themselves born, do they? I refuse to think about what might happen next. Heaven, hell, para-spiriting, whatever. Never did have that discussion about God. Bit late now because the bullet's very, very close, in fact it's kissing the blanket just below my breastbone. He's a very good shot, Habril, give him that.

I lie there and lie there. And lie there. Nothing. I hope this isn't it. Nothingness. That would be hell, wouldn't it? If there was nothing. But then I realize that I can still hear the voices of the onlookers, not loudly anymore, it's a more ordinary, more precise sound coupled with ring-tones of cell phones. They're calling the emergency services, they are making remarks about lunatics in the mall, and men collapsed on the floor and little dark-haired boys being flung about by naked thirteen-year-olds. Disgusting. No one seems to have noticed the bullet. Or lack of it.

I open my eyes.

"Give me back my baby's blanket, you pervert," says a woman in a white jogging suit. She snatches the blanket and, as she does so, I notice a small black stain on it in the shape of a ring, and with it comes a whiff of gunpowder.

Mary, back on her feet, comes over to where Akim is lying and I (without the blanket) am crouching.

"Who *are* you?" she asks.

"I know it might not seem very likely, Mary" (and she quivers when I use her real name), "but I think I'm your savior. That is a person who just saved your life. I also think I may be an Aeternal." The word chills me.

"Crazy kid," yells someone. "You're crazy."

Then attention is momentarily diverted to the upper terrace where there seems to be a scuffle going on and then the sudden ring of a second shot.

But I don't have much time to pay attention to that because, out of Debenhams, comes a woman with a dark coat and a downcast expression who is just about to negotiate her way around our group when her eyes are caught by something curled up and white on the ground. Me.

"Cassina," she yells, "oh, my God, Cassina!"

And she's sobbing well before she gets to me, well before she flings her arms about my beautiful living body and hugs me like she'll never let me go. I inhale her oh-so-familiar scent.

"Hello, Mom," I say.

16

Akim Saralli Watabi was dead. He was aware of that, looking at his body lying on the marble floor of the mall. Frantic people were trying to force their living breath into his slack mouth. Kind people, thought Akim, but misguided.

He hovered above his old self, waiting. The wings of the angel, which had seemed so loud to him only a moment before, had quietened. In fact, he could no longer hear the beat of wings at all. But he was not afraid; he had spent a lifetime preparing for the angel and the angel would come. As he waited, he watched the hectic doings of the people below him. He felt detached from everything and everyone, except, he realized, from Mary. Looking at her made him feel as he might feel looking at his own child. She was safe. She was alive. And he loved her. Ridiculous, how could he have come to love her in so short a time? And yet he did. Had. Life was such a strange, precious thing.

And death?

He had expected, he realized, something swift: the powerful embrace of Ingali, lifting him straight to the feet of his Lord. *Know this, Akim Watabi, your god sees all your deeds, done and undone.* Akim had loved but also murdered, so he was afraid of judgment. There were things he would have to explain. Yet he knew J'lal to be a merciful God as well as a vengeful one. He would ask for forgiveness. He would hope for nothing but to be allowed to see Manina again; Esta. That would be heaven enough for him.

But where was the angel?

What happened next was sudden and seismic. There was nothing soft or feathery about it, it was like the clashing of tectonic plates, a force of nature (or so it seemed) that propelled Akim far away from the mall: beyond city, country, continent, past the edge of the earth itself and on and on through the whole collection of planets that had been his universe. The traveling continued, galaxy beyond galaxy, until Akim arrived in a firmament without stars. He was barely out of breath. It was a dark place, but Akim felt on the brink of things. Perhaps he had expected too much too soon and now the angel would come. He waited for the sound of wings, but there were no wings. He listened for a voice or an instruction. But there was no voice and no instruction.

The second set of jolts were more intimate. It was as though the dark of the place was jostling him, squashing him up, making him into something very much smaller than he had been. At first he tried to fight the force, push back at it, but it was far too strong for him; besides, he realized with surprise that nothing of him was actually being lost. Rather the reverse, in fact. It was as though everything he'd ever been or thought or imagined or done, all of these things were being compressed together so that somehow he was becoming the sum of himself. He was a child with a slingshot at Sacrini, a father whose daughter lay dead in the dust, a widower who found comfort in the brotherhood of J'lal, a holy bomber, and also a man who had refused to shed more blood, who took a child that wasn't his and kissed her. All squashed up he was love and hate, dreams and failures, passion and quietness. He was also, he thought, unexceptional.

The time of the angel had clearly passed. It must be the time of judgment. How would he weigh in the balance? Was he a good man or a bad one? He listened with some trepidation for the footsteps of God. But no one came, and no one said a thing.

So (in the dark and the void) he waited. What else was he to do?

How long he waited he didn't know because there was nothing with which to measure time, no rising and setting of a sun, no turning of a world and therefore no seasons, no summer or winter, autumn or spring. So maybe he waited an old Earth year or maybe it was only a moment before he saw something take shape in the darkness. It was slightly paler than the darkness, but still black and crouched. It was also crying.

"And J'lal said: 'Ingali, bring me the souls of the martyrs, for it is them that I love, they will be with me in Paradise forever.'" There was a sob and then another cry: "J'lal, where are you, my god?"

And Akim, who had thought himself to be alone, trembled with joy to hear even so miserable a voice.

"Friend," he called, "friend, I am here with you."

But the crouching shape made no reply, it just continued to wail and call upon its god.

Akim wanted so much to reach out to the shape, to touch it maybe, but he had nothing with which to touch. He was, he imagined, just a shape like the one he saw before him, a concentrated presence, that was all. And yet he stayed by the howling shape, for perhaps an hour, a day, a year, hoping that their god would come and give them comfort. But there was no god and no comfort.

Eventually Akim moved away from the shape and some of the darkness dispelled then. It was as though either he hadn't been looking properly, or the howling creature had cast a double darkness about itself and so prevented him from seeing. For once Akim began to see, he realized this world was not at all as dark as he had assumed. In fact it was full of strange and vivid things. And at first he couldn't understand the forms he found about him, their shapes and colors, but then he realized that these things, too, were concentrations of themselves. So he would see raindrops, a million of them, compressed into one shining teardrop, and it would make him feel as refreshed as a shower of rain on a thundery summer's day and as choked as if he had cried for a million years.

At first it was only the small things he saw: the blades of grass, fields of them concentrated into one jewel of green; the grains of sand that had become just one grain, hard and sharp and crystalline. Later the bigger things revealed themselves: clouds that had become the palest and softest wisp of vapor, rivers like crashing silver threads, and mountain ranges with hard rock faces and tiny snowy peaks, surrounding him wholly but no bigger than him, just part of all he knew, all that had been.

So nothing, he thought, is lost. It astonished him. Nothing that had ever existed had fallen away! So when he turned and felt a sweep of happiness, he knew that he was passing a smile, or, when he felt loved, the air might be thick with kisses.

Of course there were darker places, places where sudden curses daggered through him, skewering him with fear. Or where jealousy lurked, or hate boiled and spat. These places were chaotic and unpredictable, but also sucking, like a bog. He was afraid he would go under, not because the bog would swallow him, but because there still were parts of him that were the bog.

"Manina!" he called then. "Esta!" As though they would return to him, as though his love for them would protect him.

No one answered but the howlers. There were more of them now, or maybe he just heard them more now, their lonely shrieks. Of course, as he could move at will, he could avoid these places, and for a while he did so, dedicating himself to a—fruitless—search for his wife and child. Yet something pulled him back: it was that first crouching shape. This soul seemed familiar to him, he felt he should be able to take it a smile or a kiss or a word of hope. But no matter what he brought, the shape still howled.

"*Anatarah istali batak,* my god release me!"

On one occasion that he returned to this bitter place, Akim was aware of something new by his side. A different kind of presence, small and waiting.

"Who's there?" he cried.

"It is I," said a voice, soft and cool.

And Akim felt, inside his surprise, an overwhelming gladness. He was not wholly alone, after all! He was so afraid of being alone. He knew then that if this new world with all its concentrated beauty had pressed about him, and he had been alone, it would not have been enough.

"Are there others then?" he whispered full of hope, for, of course, he meant Manina, he meant Esta.

"Yes," the presence replied. "Thousands of millions. Everyone who has ever been is here."

"But I see no one," cried Akim. "Can find no one. No one but the howlers!"

"Did you see everything when you first arrived?" the presence questioned him.

"No."

"Do you see more now?"

"Yes."

"There you are. That's how it works."

"So you've found others, spoken to them," pressed Akim, "and they've spoken back?"

"I'm speaking to you, aren't I?"

"But this one," said Akim, indicating the howler, "I speak and speak to him, I bring him things. But he never replies."

"I spoke to you many times," said the presence, "before you replied."

"Spoke to me? But I never heard you, never heard anything."

"A presence has to be ready to receive. This one here beside you is not. He is closed up, locked inside himself. He sees nothing, hears nothing, except the old life, the old ways. He is not yet ready. And you can't have been ready either. Until now."

"*Anatarah istali batak*," shrieked the howler. And his voice sounded so like Habril's.

"Why doesn't the Lord answer him?" Akim burst out then.

"Which Lord is that?" asked the presence.

"The T'lanni god. My god! The T'lanni god of this T'lanni Paradise!"

"Paradise!" the small shape laughed, a tinkling of bells, a clatter of stars. "You think that man there is in paradise? I think he's in hell. This place is paradise, and it is also hell. And it is not a T'lanni place. It is just a place. All people are here, T'lannis, Muslims, Jews, Christians, atheists . . ."

"But then there must be a god—or gods!"

"Sometimes," said the small presence, "sometimes I think I see God, but I'm not sure."

"You see Him?" cried Akim. "Where!"

"It's not a 'him,' and it may not be God at all. But it sometimes seems divine to me."

"What?" asked Akim. "I don't understand."

"The light. The spark. Look, look there!"

And Akim looked and looked, but he saw nothing at all.

"What do you mean," he said. "Where?"

"You don't see it?" the small presence asked. "You don't see any of the lights?"

"No."

The presence sighed. "Maybe it's just me after all," she (Akim was so sure the shape was female) said. "I so hoped it wasn't just me."

Akim looked again, tried to see beyond what he thought he knew. He took his mind from the bitter howler place and threw it back to the places of beauty, for surely there would be God? And then he saw something, a tiny brightness in the mountains, like a candle lit in the depths of the rock. And once he'd seen this light, he saw others, in the faraway breath of a magnolia blossom, in the blue that had been the sky, in all the tears and also the kisses. Then he brought his mind back to where he was, beside the presence, and he looked at her, too. And there it was, a small, fierce light.

"I see it," he said.

"You do?" There was such gratitude in her voice.

"I see it in you."

"And I in you," she replied.

And he looked down and within and saw then—and felt—at the heart of himself, a spark.

"Is it in everyone?" he asked.

"I think so. Look." He felt his gaze directed to the howler. At the very center of the darkness was a tiny, guttering flame.

"So he will be all right!" cried Akim. "He, too, will be all right."

"Perhaps. Perhaps not. He carries the flame, but he has yet to find it. Who knows whether he will or not?"

"But if he cannot find it, his god surely will. His god will find him here."

"Has your god found you here?" asked the presence.

That silenced Akim.

"Who are you?" he asked at last.

"Just a child," the presence replied. "At least I was a child."

"I had a child," Akim cried. "Esta. She died. And Manina, her mother. They must be here. I have to find them. Can you help me with that? Do you know how to find people?"

"It's not that easy," said the presence quietly.

"What?"

"It's not the way of this world. You want your daughter, you want your wife because they were the most to you, you loved them more than anyone else, more than anything else, more than life itself, yes?"

"Yes, of course."

"Here, to move on, you will need to love everyone so."

"Everyone! Love everyone as I loved them! Love you and that howler as I loved my own wife and child? Impossible. I couldn't do it. I couldn't cope. I'd burst with loving!"

"Then you won't move on," said the presence simply. "You won't hear, and you won't be heard."

Then Akim thought of Mary and how he had loved her.

"This, Akim," continued the presence, "is a different world."

"Akim! Akim; you know my name?"

"There are things you tell me, Akim, with your speech, and things you tell me with your presence. You are new here. You, too, will learn to know."

"Then tell me who you are, what is your name, tell me that at least."

"My name is Aelfin."

"Aelfin Dixon? The child of the bomb?"

"The child of your bomb, Akim."

"Oh, Aelfin." And Akim felt in need of knees, if he had

knees he would fall to them. "Can you forgive me? Can you forgive me, Aelfin?"

"Forgive you?" said Aelfin. "That is not a request that has any meaning now. It is down to you. You need to forgive yourself. Do you forgive yourself, Akim?"

A silence, like the one before a judgment.

"Akim?"

17

I'm sitting up in my bedroom with my body and my clothes on. I'm getting used to the body; I'm not quite so clumpy anymore, though I do bang into the odd basin. My eyesight and my hearing have returned to normal, too, although perhaps I shouldn't use the word *normal*, which has begun to take on difficult connotations for me. Perhaps I should just say, I see and hear as I did before, before that first bomb, before Akim, before my life changed.

I'm up here alone, but I will not be alone for long. It's four months since my homecoming but my mother still comes upstairs to touch me. She pretends that she's collecting washing, or needs to ask me a "quick question," but actually she wants to check if I'm still here, if I remain, exist. And I understand that impulse, so I just let her. She might brush my shoulder as she passes, touch my cheek, take my hand, in hers or simply gaze—and gaze—at me.

"You'll suffocate her," my father says.

"She's my miracle, my miracle child," my mother cries. "I prayed, and God answered those prayers. How can I not be grateful? Besides," my mother adds in a low voice, "you know . . ."

But nobody does quite. The general view is that I have had some sort of breakdown.

"And wouldn't you?" my mother says to her friend Pam. "If you'd seen what Cassina has seen?"

I need, apparently, a great deal of support, of constant, loving care, to return me to "normal."

It was my fault, of course, for beginning with the truth. I cheerfully told my parents about going up beyond the known universe and then being concentrated into a small ball of mist. I explained about the nature of para-spirits, the rules and regulations, I even gave Dad a brief on Blacoe, the old schoolmasterly para who inhabits his brain.

"Oh," said Dad. "Right."

"You don't believe me?"

"Er . . ."

I decided to conduct an experiment; the problem was it relied on Blacoe being cooperative. "Right, Blacoe," I said, "I know you can hear me. Please come out a moment. Just put yourself by Dad's right cheek. That's right as you look out of his face. Dad's right. He'll feel wet," I said to Dad. "Not very wet, just like a kind of damp patch on your skin. It'll only be for a moment and then he'll have to go back in your brain, else he'll dry out."

Actually even saying it aloud made me feel fairly stupid. And then there was Dad's face; it looked sad and contorted.

"Feel anything?" I asked, after a moment.

"No," said Dad. "Not really." He exchanged a look with Mom.

"Grumpy old stick," I said.

"What?" said Dad.

"Blacoe. Thanks for nothing, pal." I don't think the guy understands the notion of friendship.

I changed tactics. I gave my parents a detailed lesson on the structure of the cerebellum. I described the precise location of the fissure, the shape of the central lobes, indicated the part of the brain where memory seems to be situated, and then I gave them a quick tour of the heart, paying particular attention to the exact positions of the arteries and veins entering and leaving this major organ. There was a short pause and then Dad said, "Top-class biology teacher you've got." After that I tried sharing with Mom some facts about my birth which I could only have known from being inside her head and she said, "I'm so glad I made you that photo album, darling."

Fact-blindness. That's what I've decided to call this phenomenon. You give someone incontrovertible proof of something, and they still persist in telling you that an A road is a B road. I gave up then. Mom and Dad didn't give up; they felt I should see a shrink.

Dr. Jonathan Wellbottom was quite interested in my case. He'd done some research on schizophrenics which proved that some people who heard voices could be helped with hypnosis. The "spirit" inhabiting the head could be called upon during hypnosis to declare itself. It could be asked for its life story and questioned about why it was troubling the subject. Most spirits apparently talked about jolts in cars and going down long, dark corridors and "getting stuck" and "feeling trapped." When asked by sympathetic doctor whether they saw any way out of their predicament, the spirit might reply that he "could see a door" and then all the great hypno had to do then was steer him through that door (presumably into some proper death) and slam it shut behind him.

"Do you experience such voices?" Dr. Wellbottom asked.

I mentioned to Dr. Wellbottom that he seemed to have got the wrong end of the stick: I was the spirit which had been doing the haunting and, far from going through a door to death, I seemed to have come back through one marked Life. I even told him the bit about exploding back into flesh, because I thought, being a scientific man, he might find it interesting. Dr. Wellbottom remained calm throughout, and then confided to my parents that there were a number of personality disorders suggested by my particular symptoms and certain excellent drugs which, with a few minimal side effects, could help with the delusions.

It was at that point that I admitted defeat. I conceded that I'd been confused and dazed and had wandered about and lost track of time and just made up the para-spirit story to explain why I hadn't come home immediately.

"I wanted to come home," I said to Mom. "I really did." Which, of course, was true. "Only I couldn't seem to find my way."

This explanation was simple and acceptable. I was hugged, hugged, and hugged again, and also forgiven. Dr. Wellbottom was declared a quack and a waste of money. I was glad but also irritated. I thought how very narrow-minded people are. Anything that doesn't quite fit the pattern and it's "abnormal," "untrue." I wondered how many fabulous things there are in the universe which we fail to notice because our wits are too dim?

"Post-traumatic stress disorder," said Dad. "Exactly what I said in the first place."

"You never said anything of the sort," said Mom.

"Well, I'm saying it now," said Dad.

Dad also had a problem with the funeral people.

"I mean, who was in that coffin? What or who exactly did they charge us for? I'm going to write a letter. They're not getting away with that. It's outrageous."

My mom said just to leave it. "We got our daughter back, didn't we? Who cares whose body's in the coffin?"

"The family of that person," exclaimed Dad.

Eventually Mom came up with a "rational" explanation for that, too.

"Probably bits and bobs of other people, already decently buried. There must have been so many body parts," said Mom. "You can't DNA every fingernail."

"Of course you can," said Dad. "In fact you must."

Mom won then because she burst into tears and the word *Aelfin* hung unsaid in the air and Dad had to shut up. But Dad had the final victory because, as my miraculous return from the dead was all over the newspapers, the funeral parlor felt obliged to send an ex-gratia payment and a letter which talked about "tightening up procedures."

Did you notice how I slipped in the bit about the newspapers? I was in the newspapers. Not just the local rag (double-page spread) but in the nationals. A good half page in *The Times* and an entire photo extravaganza in the *Mail* and half a dozen other tabloids, too. "Back from the Dead," screamed the headlines. If only they knew! Reporters with long lenses were camped outside our door again. They didn't need the long lenses because I was quite happy to go outside and give them a generous full-faced smile. Mom said it would be better not to mention the para-spirit business, so I didn't, though I might have got more column inches that way. Anyhow, as a result Mom has had to devote an entire suitcase to the clippings, so I can't complain. Although the accounts were not quite as accurate as I would have wanted.

No one noticed my heroism.

This is what is generally agreed to have happened: Akim had a heart attack (yeah, right) and Habril was foiled by our enormously vigilant secret service. Turned out there was some intelligence that the mall was a target, and the place was crawling with undercover special agents. Habril had only just managed to get his gun out and fire the shot when they were on to him—literally, physically; that was the scuffle I heard. Of course, being Habril, he wasn't exactly going to give in gracefully so they shot him. Shot him dead. "Resisting arrest" and "endangering the public" were phrases bandied about; but I think they just wanted to shoot him, so they did.

Habril's bullet, the one I took on my own naked-but-for-a-baby-blanket chest, was assumed to have gone astray, embedding itself safely in some post or wall or piece of flooring, as yet unfound. "No one was hurt"—that was the main thing.

Only I was hurt and Mary, too, and also Akim and Habril. I'm having trouble believing Akim and Habril are both dead. But then maybe they're not, maybe one of them is, even now, holed up in my brain as a para-spirit. How would I know? It's an uncomfortable thought. Hello, Akim; hello, Habril. Are you there? I mean, here? No, I think they're gone; Akim certainly, he looked so—final—somehow, lying on the floor of the mall. I felt sorry for him. And it wasn't just because Mary was battering me with her little fists, I felt sorry right inside myself. And of course I also thought—maybe I'd misjudged him.

Maybe he never intended to take Mary to Paradise after all. Because he might have known, might have worked it out, that time in the desert when he was only five and Padua threw herself across him, kissed him. He survived and she didn't: she died. So maybe that was it, maybe he knew that if he kissed Mary, she would live, become an Aeternal, and he would die, history would repeat itself. Maybe the bomb was not in the equation, he never intended to detonate it at all. And me, little old Cassina Dixon, I just shoved myself in the way and changed what was to be. But you have to act sometimes, don't you? If you care about things, about other people, about the world, you have to act.

Which brings me to the matter of feelings: how do I feel about Akim being dead? Well, there were times when I'd have cheerfully killed him myself; tried to really, that occasion when I tightened myself around his heart. But it's a bit more complicated now. I'm not sad exactly, but I wish he wasn't gone. I'd like to have had the opportunity to talk to him, listen to him, argue with him. I feel he never really spoke up. But then his actions spoke, I suppose. And I'm going to choose to believe that he would never have detonated that second bomb, that his intention was only to save Mary. I'm going to believe that. I think it's called faith. As for whether I forgive him—if not for my death then for Aelfin's—I haven't quite worked that out yet. Maybe I do forgive him, maybe I don't, maybe it's not my place to judge anyway—only to try and understand. And, having done a tour of duty in his brain, I think I do understand more now, a bit more. Maybe that has to be enough.

As for Habril, Habril's more difficult for me, because even though his mother died at the Southern Gate, I don't think his motives were ever really personal; which is not to say his motives weren't genuine, far from it. I believe he really cared about the big things: his people, his culture, his God. His intentions were good even if he didn't exactly go about things in a humane way. I keep remembering Padua's remark about the soft shoes; in fact those soft shoes haunt me. "If you haven't stood in the soft shoes of those pushed down, if you don't look at the world through their eyes, just once . . . then you haven't done enough." But I'm still glad he's gone. There, I've said it. Because imagining is a two-way street, isn't it? And Habril never bothered to stand in my shoes. Or Aelfin's. Or Mary's.

I think about Padua, too, of course, and what she'll do, where she'll go, now that Akim and Habril are gone. And even though she could be infuriating and preachy, I find myself feeling sorry for her, sorry about her. But then maybe, having to get a new host, maybe that will move her on a bit. Who will she choose? The head of the special-agent officer who shot her son dead? That would be a test of forgiveness for sure. Or maybe the head of some random shopper? Would that be easier or harder for her? I don't know, though sometimes I think Padua's journey might be to stop being the mother of the boy who went bad. Because in the end each one of us, man, woman, and child, we have to take responsibility for ourselves, don't we? Start over, start again. Just like I'm having to right now.

All this fine talk about the fate of other people—do you know why I'm doing it? To stop me thinking about myself, the frightening prospect of being an Aeternal. Padua was right about that, too. It is quite a lot to take in. Of course I've tried to look at it positively: Weh hey! I'm invulnerable; I'm Superman; well, Supergirl anyway. And being a hero—a heroine—wasn't that what I always wanted? If I want to jump down mountain crevasses or chuck myself out of airplanes without a parachute, I can do it. I can offer myself to the French Foreign Legion, infiltrate the Mafia with impunity, be the only war correspondent who doesn't have to wear a bulletproof vest.

Or can I?

You see, no one's exactly given me the handbook for being an Aeternal. In fact I only have Padua's word, and what I observed from Akim, that there really is such a state. I mean, what if you only get to be invulnerable if someone's actually shooting at you? So if you abandon your parachute or fall under a bus, that's your own lookout. Or what if it's only bullets and bombs you have protection from, but not knives or poison? Or perhaps there's a time limit, you only have so many lives, so four bullets is fine, but five is curtains? Russian roulette. Who's to know, who's to say?

As for being chosen, no, I do not feel chosen. Dumped on, perhaps. Like, whose great idea was this anyway? Uh-oh, I feel God creeping in again here, the guy who's in charge. Well, what if actually no one's in charge? What if it's just me in charge? Have to schedule time to think about that.

And what about old age? Can I be killed by diseases or

not? Imagine if all my friends got older and older—and eventually died—and I was left behind. Still here, still getting older. That makes me realize a strange thing, that death is part of life. If you were denied death, I don't think you could say you'd really lived, not fully, not completely. Because death—well, it's part of the journey, part of what makes us human. The last big adventure.

Then there's the passing on of this blessing—this curse. I had some bad moments about the kissing aspect, I can tell you. I thought if the moment I kiss someone they get to be an Aeternal and I drop dead, it doesn't augur well for teenage romance, does it? Then I remembered that I'd already kissed Bonnie, and Mom and Dad, so it can't be just a kiss. I've decided it must be a kiss in a life-threatening situation, that's what transfers the Aeternal scourge. Like Padua kissing five-year-old Akim in the desert when the soldier's bullet was coming, or Akim trying to kiss Mary in the mall when Habril's bullet was coming. But I could be wrong. Not knowing makes me edgy, but I've decided to look at that positively, too. That's what I've learned, I suppose; that things could change tomorrow. And not just a little bit, cataclysmically. So I think the only thing to do is this: Grab life now, hold it, hug it, squeeze it dry, because tomorrow—who knows about tomorrow? I've also learned something about acting, not up on stage but in the drama of your own life. Spending all that time as a para-spirit, when I couldn't change a thing, couldn't make a difference, has made me realize how precious our ability to intervene, to act, to speak out really is. I guess I was never the sort of kid who stood back from things; but now I feel it's a credo: I will step forward; I will do whatever is in my power to make things better. And I will try to stand in other people's shoes.

Every journey begins with a single step—which is why

I went to see Mary, just before Christmas. My mother couldn't understand it at all.

"Why would you want to see that poor kidnap kid? You only met her in the mall for five minutes. What can you possibly have to say to her or her to you?"

I wasn't really in a position to explain that.

"You don't even know her address," Mom said.

"Thirty-three Kilne Road," I said. And then, seeing that familiar twitch and panic in my mother, I added, "She said it over and over, like a mantra. I think it was the fear."

My father took his nose out of some self-help manual he was reading and suggested Mom let me go because it might help me with "closure."

"Let her go?" my mom said. "I'm not letting her out of my sight."

So she came with me. We telephoned in advance, of course. Mom got the number from the book. She explained herself to Mrs. Laney and, of course, Mrs. Laney said that was fine. Mrs. Laney said she often had people to tea.

It was strange going back to the apartment, being the one to actually press the elevator button, watching Mrs. Laney open the door, looking at her face to face.

"Cassina Dixon," she said, "pleased to meet you. Welcome to my home."

I would have liked to say I could give her a tour of her apartment with my eyes shut, describe the configuration of the rooms, the layout of her kitchen, the size and dimensions of her Christmas tree. But that would only have upset my mother, so I kept quiet.

Aunt Lou was wearing a pink suit with navy piping on it and free-fall face powder. She stared at me: "Do I know you?" she asked.

"Of course not," said Mrs. Laney. "Cassina, Mrs. Dixon, this is my aunt Lou."

"I'm sure I know you," said Aunt Lou.

And I was really tempted to say, "Ax-murderer," but I didn't.

Mary sat on the floor beneath the huge, and now fully decorated, Christmas tree. Instead of an angel at the top, there was a star made of tinfoil. While Mrs. Laney fussed about tea and cakes and Aunt Lou eyed me suspiciously, I went to sit beside Mary.

"I like your tree," I said.

Mary said nothing. Her mouth was set, and she shuffled backward, away from me.

"Did you make the star yourself?"

No answer.

"It's lovely," I said, and then I added, "but I liked your other tree better. The newspaper one. With the angel."

She tilted her head to one side. Her hair was still cropped and black, as though Habril had only just that moment chopped it. But back in her own home, with her own things about her, she didn't look abused, just boyish, elfin.

"Who are you?" she asked.

"One of the bomb dead," I replied, and it was nice to be able to smile at her. "Cassina Dixon. You put me on that tree."

"But you're alive," she said.

"Yes," I said. "And so are you. Funny old world."

"Akim's not alive," she said softly.

"Ax-murderer," piped up Aunt Lou from the opposite side of the room.

"Aunt Lou . . .," began Mrs. Laney. "Please don't mind my aunt. Biscuit, anyone?"

My mother had a biscuit.

"I'm sorry about pushing you away, pushing you to the ground in the mall," I said. "But I didn't kill Akim." I paused. "I didn't save you, either. I think Akim did that." I wanted to say, *In fact I think he gave his life for you;* but that's quite a heavy thing to bear, so I just added, "He cared about you. I know he did."

For the first time Mary looked me in the face. "He didn't let me fall," she said. "He promised he would hold me and he did."

"Yes. Like in your dream."

She stared then. "I don't dream that dream anymore. It's gone away."

"Because of Akim?"

"No. Because of Dad. He's come back. After, after . . . they took me, took me away, he came back. He's promised to see me. Every week. And after Christmas I'm going to stay there. At his place." There was a snort from Aunt Lou on the other side of the room, but Mary's eyes were shining.

"I'm so glad," I said.

"So there is a God," Mary said. "There must be, after all."

I had nothing to say to that, so I kept quiet.

"Hallelujah," said Mrs. Laney.

"Bit weird, that family," said Mom in the car home, and then, a bit later, "Are you all right, darling?"

"Yes," I said. I don't think we will be seeing the Laneys again, but I've said what I needed to to Mary. And I think Mary will be all right. And I find I care about that.

I get up and go into Aelfin's room. I spend quite a lot of time in here. It's April now, nearly Easter. At Christmas Mom put all Aelfin's Christmas presents under the tree. There was no tree when I came home, but we did go together, Dad and Mom and me and Bonnie to get our tree from the parking-lot man. He congratulated Mom on the return of her daughter; he'd read it in the papers, of course, which made it all the more stark that Aelfin wasn't there. It was a bleak trip home. But we did the decorations, and Mom put out Aelfin's presents.

"One miracle," she said. "Why not two?"

"Because," said my father.

"Because what?"

"Because it would be too much."

I'm not exactly sure what he meant by that, but I think he meant too much joy. As though he didn't, he couldn't, deserve it.

After Christmas Mom put Aelfin's still-wrapped presents in her room.

"Just in case."

In March, Dad put them in the attic, and Mom didn't get cross with him, so things are changing, slowly.

I've kept quiet about going inside Aelfin's body. I don't think my parents would like the idea of that. But I remember that sense of it being a violin case without a violin in it, and I don't think Aelfin's coming back. I still can't help myself whispering her name, when I'm close by people she loved, or who loved her, in case she's a para-spirit, in case she can come out and, just for a moment, touch my cheek. But she never comes, which is why I sit in her room sometimes and touch her things, touch things she once touched. It doesn't make things better, of course, but it does make me feel less bereft.

I loved that girl, really I did. My sister.

I sit here and wonder about where she's gone, where she is right now and if she's okay. So it may have come; yes, I think it has. I think I'm finally going to have that conversation with myself about God.

18

Aelfin Filide Dixon stayed beside the presence of her murderer. Since she had asked him: "Do you forgive yourself?" he had lost his voice. He could no longer speak, only howl. She blamed herself, it was a question she shouldn't have asked. Who was she to play God?

So she stayed with him, whispering words of comfort and apology, but he did not respond. Time became timelessness. Things went on, but they didn't change. Sometimes Aelfin felt angry—she was trying hard and what was he doing? Sometimes she felt frustrated: she knew, in order to move on in this new world, she was supposed to love this presence, but how? There was even one time when she felt she might give up. And yet, even in death, she remained a child, carried a little bursting hope inside her. He would respond, *he would*, all she had to do was find something more to give. But what?

She decided on quietness, sat beside him with a clear space in her soul which she hoped he might fill with needs of his own. As she waited, and waited, gradually she realized he was leaning—oh so slightly—toward the light in her. Maybe this was his longing? She moved toward him, used the light inside herself to touch him, as though she was a spill and he a match. She saw at once how her brightness increased his—though only a tiny bit, and it was painful to her, for the fire that she gave him (even though she gave it willingly) seemed to diminish her, leaving her breathless and smothered. She was frightened then, for she understood that it would be possible to give him everything and be left with nothing for herself. Her own light was not infinite. She could go out like a candle and then what?

So she pulled away from Akim, keeping her light for herself, letting her flame grow fat again. Who knows for how long she left him? She took herself far enough away not to hear his howls. He'd snuffed out her life once. Was she to allow him to snuff it out again?

But either her curiosity—or perhaps her care—made her want to return to him. There was no one in this place with whom she had a more intimate bond. But when she came to the place where she thought she had left him, he wasn't there.

"Akim," she cried, but there was no reply, not even a howl.

"Akim!" It frightened her, the silence. "Answer me, Akim!"

From somewhere, close by, there came a weak, dried-up croak. It was a more horrible sound than any of his howls. And it was him, she was sure of it. She felt him—but where was he? She scanned the murkiness about her: shadows, shadows, nothing but shadows. And yet she felt him still. Had Akim become so dim he was now indistinguishable from the dark?

"Akim," she cried in her mind, "find me."

But he could not. So she searched for him, searched and would not give up. Finally she found the last tiny sputter of him, the spark that hadn't quite gone out.

She flung herself at him then, pressing her burning heart against him, lighting him again with her own flame. She saw at once how he sucked on her light; how, as he grew stronger and brighter, her own light faded, and yet, this time, she did not pull away.

"Aelfin," she heard him whisper, and she was astonished at his voice, his quickened strength.

Good-bye, Akim, she wanted to say but she was too weak to speak.

"Aelfin," he called again. "Oh, my Aelfin." And in that word *my* was a rush of wind. It blew in and around her so that out of that last darkness burst a new flame, wilder and more joyous than anything she'd ever known before. And whether Akim had passed her back the light, or whether there was a part of her that could never be extinguished, or whether, at last, she was in the presence of something other and holy, she couldn't tell. All she knew for certain was that she felt like living touch-paper and that, together, she and Akim were powerful enough to light this whole universe. In fact, they were lighting this whole universe!

Or so she thought.

In truth, the sudden, brilliant light about them was far too bright to be hers and Akim's alone. There were bursts of light to east and west, north and south. For the first time the rim of this world was illumined. She could see a horizon.

And the horizon pulled her—and the whole host of others who (she began to understand) were also making the light. And maybe these others, this huge multitude, had been beside her all the while, and she'd never seen them.

"Come on," she called to Akim, full of voice now. "Come on!"

She shouted with the excitement of someone who'd found a whole new universe to explore.

But Akim never moved at all. The light scared him. What if the brightness was not the light of J'lal (for which he had been preparing all his life) but the light of the child? Not the light of his god but the light of her good, and the good in all the other souls here with them? For wasn't it Aelfin and her dogged, generous love who had changed things?

Akim was afraid because, if he was right, there was indeed a whole new universe in front of them; and if it was only goodness that mattered, goodness which carried no reward but itself, then they really were alone.

Which is why he waited, why he hung back.

"Come on," she called again. "Come on!"

And he wanted to warn her of what was ahead, because after all she was only a child, and she, too, had hoped for the divine.

"What are you waiting for?" she cried.

He was waiting for another truth. One less hard than this perhaps. He was also thinking of Habril.

"Habril," said Aelfin, hooking into his mind, "will come—if he comes—when he's ready." She paused. "But your time is now."

"You know the future then?" Akim asked.

"No. Of course not. But I know when it's time to begin. It's time now, Akim."

The others were going. So many, many others. Surely that was a comfort?

"Please, Akim."

Besides, he owed Aelfin, owed her her life and also his own, but it didn't seem to be about that anymore. It seemed to be about something altogether bigger, and he just didn't know if he was up to it.

"Akim?"

"Yes," he replied, at last. "I'm coming."

Acknowledgments

The Innocent's Story was an easy book to write—not in terms of putting the words on the page—but in terms of knowing, after 9/11, what I needed to write about, what I needed to try and understand. It's been a complex book to publish and I'm profoundly grateful to Oxford University Press for their sensitivity, their judgment, and their unwavering belief that challenging issues can and should be brought to young people. I have particularly valued the energetic criticism and support of Liz Cross, Polly Nolan, and Kate Williams. Many people read the book in manuscript; of these I pay special tribute to Noga Applebaum. As someone who has lost family to terrorists, she has more right than most to be entrenched. I found her sharp, open-minded, and wise. I thank Gillie Russell for her many good suggestions and Peter Tabern, whose cogent understanding of story has made this a better one. I'm grateful to Father David of All Saints Church, Hove, England, who lent me books and talked to me about God when he was supposed to be making pancakes. Any errors or atheisms are mine. I thank undertaker James Whittle and embalmer Geoff Taylor, who led me through the world of the dead. That's a different sort of unafraid.

And finally, for being her dogged, tough, loving, generous self, I remain forever indebted to my agent, Clare Conville.